The Crime on Cote des Neiges

The Crime on Cote des Neiges

David Montrose

A Ricochet Book

Véhicule Press

Published with the generous assistance of the Canada
Council for the Arts, the Book Publishing Industry
Development Program of the Department of Canadian
Heritage, and the Société de développement des entreprises
culturelles du Québec (SODEC).

Adaptation of original cover: J.W. Stewart
Consulting editor: Brian Busby
Special assistance: Claire Grandy
Printed by Marquis Printing Inc.

LIBRARY AND ARCHIVES CANADA CATALOGUING
IN PUBLICATION
Montrose, David, 1920-1968
The Crime on Cote des Neiges / David Montrose.
(Ricochet)
Originally published in 1951.

ISBN 978-1-55065-284-0

I. Title. II. Series: Ricochet (Véhicule Press)
PS8513.R2C75 2010   C813'.54   C2010-900778-6

Published by Véhicule Press, Montréal, Québec, Canada
www.vehiculepress.com

Distribution in Canada by LitDistCo
www.litdistco.ca

Distributed in the U.S. by Independent Publishers Group
www.ipgbook.com

Printed in Canada on recycled paper

Publisher's Note (2010)

This is a new edition of the long out-of-print *The Crime on Cote des Neiges* which was published in 1951. It is the first book in the Véhicule Press Ricochet series. Typos that appeared in the original book have been corrected; the sexist and racist attitudes of the period remain.

Foreword to the 2010 Edition

DAVID MONTROSE belongs to a select group that includes novelist Brian Moore, newspaperman Al Palmer and transplanted Englishman Martin Brett—writers who six decades ago brought pulp noir to Montreal. That they did is of no surprise; at the time, Canada's great metropolis had an international reputation as a wide open city. It was a place of booze and broads, gambling and graft, the very elements of the frowned-upon pulp fiction that cluttered paperback racks of newsstands and drugstores. If anything, the mining of Montreal's dark underbelly was overdue.

Montrose, though, was not the first to pick up shovel and pen – that prize went to Palmer, with *Sugar-Puss on Dorchester Street* – but he did come close. Published two years later, in 1951, *The Crime on Cote de Neiges* is much the superior book. It introduces Russell Teed, a private investigator specializing in bland cases of corporate embezzlement and fraud. His new job, instigated by Westmount matron Martha Scaley, is something else altogether, throwing our hero into a criminal world of violence and death. Teed is confronted with corpses, but it's nothing that he hasn't seen before; the man is, after all, a veteran of the Second World War.

What else can we say about this oddly-named private investigator? While he doesn't fit the man of mystery mould, glimpses of his past are as rare as they are fleeting. Montrose doesn't tell us much. Teed has little time for sentiment or reflection; fuelled by beer – preferably Dow, though Molson's will do – he races through the present. When the private investigator remembers to eat, it's "a good steak dinner" at Slitkin's and Slotkin's, the legendary Dorchester Street bar and grill that would later make its way into novels by Morley Callaghan and Mordecai Richler.

Sixty years on, once vibrant Dorchester Street, the center of Montreal nightlife, has been reduced to a renamed soulless boulevard. While the private detective drives his Riley roadster through a city that has receded into memory, those who experienced the metro-polis at mid-century may on occasion find something slightly unusual in these pages.

Teed's apartment building, 3945 Cote des Neiges, doesn't exist, nor does the Canam Building, where he has his office. The Scaley mansion is on Belmont Terrace, not Belmont Avenue, and pal Alan MacArnold works the police beat for *The Clarion*, not *The Gazette*. These are minor changes, designed to protect the innocent, perhaps. Others, such as mention of convicted murderer Louis Berkovitch as 'Louie Berkovitz,' appear to be nothing more than simple errors.

The most jarring disparity between fiction and fact concerns the absence of French. True, *The Crime on Cote des Neiges* preceded the Quiet Revolution by nearly a decade, but Montrose's Montreal is overwhelmingly Anglo, as it is in Teed's further adventures in *Murder Over Dorval* (1952) and in *Body on Mount Royal* (1953).

The only French Canadian character, police detective Raoul Framboise, isn't such a bad sort, even if he is a bit free with his fists. He certainly comes off better than most. Montrose follows pulp convention, giving us a city in which altruism is unknown and cynicism runs high. For

Teed, its selfish, untrustworthy women are of interest only for their bodies, and even then he's wary that any appeal is the result of 'a good corset-smith'.

Anyone looking for autobiographical elements in the Russell Teed novels will scramble. Where the private detective is the product of a privileged Westmount upbringing, Montrose was a Maritimer. Born in 1920 New Brunswick, raised in Nova Scotia, his real name was Charles Ross Graham. With a degree in Science from Dalhousie in hand, he moved to Montreal in 1941, taking up post-graduate studies at McGill University. There was a stint with the Canadian Army Operational Research Group during the Second World War, followed by studies at Harvard, where he earned his *artium magister* in Economics.

A chemical analyst, economist and university lecturer, Graham appears to have been well-positioned for the post-war world. Just how he got along is difficult to determine; Graham was a stranger to Montreal's literary circles, and his work was ignored by the local papers. What we do know is that by 1967, the year of Expo, he'd suffered the death of one wife and was in the process of divorcing a second. Graham attempted a new life as a freelance writer in Toronto, where he penned essays for the Canadian Life Insurance Association. Collected in a slim, awkwardly-titled book, *Sunshine Sketches of a Little Economics*, it would be the only publication to appear under his name.

After a break of fifteen years, Graham returned to fiction with the completion of a fourth David Montrose book. Like his previous novels, *Gambling with Fire* is set in Montreal, though our man Teed is nowhere to be found.

Readers are presented with a new hero, displaced Austrian aristocrat Franz Loebek. Graham died when *Gambling with Fire* was at press. It arrived in bookstores in early 1969, its dust jacket maintaining that the author is "living in Toronto".

Would that it was so…would that Graham had lived to write more David Montrose novels.

Fifty-nine years have passed since *The Crime on Cote des Neiges* first appeared on those wire racks. This new edition, marking the debut of the Ricochet Books series of pulp fiction reprints, appears none too soon. A scarce book, at the time of this writing, no copies were being offered by online booksellers; only four libraries in the country have it in their holdings. My thanks to Jim Fitzpatrick, who generously gave me one of his.

Brian Busby

Scene One

THE HOUSES OF WESTMOUNT climb a big, green, expensive hill and look down on Montreal. Only old families live in upper Westmount; the money to buy a place up there isn't accumulated in less than two generations. Once upon a time, the wealthy families of English Montreal lived in the upper part of the city itself, in an area called the Square Mile. Westmount was just a frowsy forested hill, and they gave away lots up there. Once upon a time some Indians gave away Manhattan for a few bottles of whiskey. Times have changed.

The greater the altitude, the deeper the tone of awe in the realtor's voice. Social eminence is measured by how much of the city flows like a pasteboard panorama out under the drawing room windows. And if one house in Westmount saw more of Montreal than any other, it was the Scaley eyrie.

I went up one of those narrow Westmount streets that tack back and forth against the mountain like a sailboat trying to make distance against a heavy wind. When I got near the top I had to breathe deeply, and the motor was gasping in the thin air. The altimeter said I was 500 feet above Westmount Boulevard. A road to the right led through the underbrush to the Scaley back door.

For fifty yards, I drove through uninhabited territory.

The car lights picked out heavy branches overhanging the road. I had the top down and once I had to duck to keep a maple bough from etching my scalp. This forest belonged to the Scaleys. When I was a kid I used to think bears lived in it. We never found one when we played there, but I still wouldn't like to walk through it at night.

Then the branches parted and I saw the house, three storeys of brown brick stacked above the sidewalk. It was a little smaller than Casa Loma in Toronto and it didn't have a moat or drawbridge, but some of King George's palaces are less impressive. There was a light on over the back door, which was really the front door because the other side of the house was flush with the face of a cliff. They were expecting me. Maybe they were even going to let me in the house, after twenty years. I used to play with Inez Scaley that long ago, but then I lived one level down in Westmount and I never did get into the house. I never got farther than the garage on a rainy day.

I parked my Riley roadster beside the door and got out. I walked around the car and across the sidewalk to the door. Warmth built up inside me and the sweat that had been poised just beneath my skin sprang out, even from that little effort. Here on top of Westmount it wasn't as bad as in the city. But it was still August.

I gave the doorbell one short ring and a little man in a white coat opened it quickly, as if he'd been connected in circuit with the bell and had felt a shock. He was old but not wrinkled, with a tight pink scalp shining through the grey hair, neat ears, a thin nose and chin and no jowls at all. His eyes were chocolate brown and calm as mud puddles on a windless day. He looked cool. Perhaps he'd been sitting on an ice cake in the cellar.

"Mrs. Scaley," I said.

He didn't ask me who I was or whether I was expected. I'll say that much for my tailor.

"She is still at dinner, sir. Will you come this way?"

He had a voice that matched the eyes, light in timbre but impressive because it was unhurried and very clear. He led me through the walnut-panelled foyer to a small room on the right.

"I'm sure Mrs. Scaley won't be long, sir," he said. "Could I get you a drink?"

I shook my head. "I just finished my own dinner," I told him. I got up and walked around the room once, dragging my ankles through the pile of the Oriental. It was a square room, too dark and not dark enough to be interesting. I sat down again and pulled out a pack of State Express and lit one; I sat and sweated.

The sweat was from the August heat, not from nervousness. There was nothing to be nervous about. Mrs. Martha Scaley had called me up to offer me a job, and in a sense I was here to sell myself. But it was out of the line of my usual work and I wasn't sure I wanted a job at all at the moment. If the heat wave was going to hang on, all I wanted was to be on top of a small mountain three miles north of Ste. Adele, where I owned a ski shack.

The house was silent while I waited for her. Silent, because all the floors were shrouded with the lifework of a score of eastern weavers. Silent, because there was almost no one living in the great rock pile. The Scaleys had been a top family in Montreal for three generations, but now only Martha was left. Her sole seed was Inez, who had married and moved away. God knew what would happen to the place when Martha died. The area was restricted, so she couldn't bequeath it to McGill for a residence or to the Salvation Army for an unwed mothers' retreat. And no one bought houses this big to live in any more—partly because the little man in the white coat was one of a dying race.

He came in again, just then, loaded to the eyebrows with a coffee tray that would have made me stagger. He carried it as though it was light as a hat box. The central piece on the tray was a towering flagon-shaped antique silver pot wrought by Fragères or Cellini, and there were the silver accessories to match and two demi-tasses and two liqueur glasses.

"How nice," I said. "We can have our coffee together while I wait for Mrs. Scaley."

He didn't ruffle worth a damn. "I beg your pardon for serving the coffee before Mrs. Scaley arrived, Sir," he said calmly. "I thought she had already come down to the study."

He went out and she came in.

Martha Scaley was short, but not lumpy. She had the same figure she'd had twenty years ago, and probably twenty years before that. She might have been corseted in a steel jacket that needed a power winch to tighten the laces, but it looked natural. She wore an absolutely plain black dress of wool finer than cashmere and crisper than spun nylon, with just enough jewels to show she wasn't in mourning.

"Good evening, Mr. Teed," she said in a voice that was by way of a Swiss finishing school and from ten years of talking with cultured men.

"Good evening, Mrs. Scaley. You used to call me Russell."

She smiled. She sat down behind the coffee pot and pushed me back into my chair with a half-inch gesture of a smooth white hand. "That was a good many years ago. You've grown up. And grown up very well, too." Her dark eyes surveyed me.

I blushed, the way I once did at a Freshman ball when

the Dean's wife told me I danced well. Everybody I talked to in this house made me feel younger. If Inez walked in later I'd ask her to come out in the garage and play jacks with me.

Martha began squirting coffee in the demi-tasses. They were bone china so thin and translucent the hot coffee should have dissolved them. I cleared my throat. The only way I could save any face was by getting down to business.

"You called me about an anonymous letter?"

"Yes," she said, but she dropped it with that. "I believe I'll have Cointreau with my coffee, Russell. Would you get it, please, from the cabinet beside the desk? And bring whatever liqueur you prefer."

Cointreau, in a plain square bottle, the straightest, most honest liqueur bottle there is. I found the bottle and brought it back. "I'd like Cointreau too," I said, and filled the puny little glasses.

We sat and drank our drams of coffee black and let the dry, satiny Cointreau roll back over our tongues. She took a Pall Mall from the big brass box and I took one too, to be polite. It was the first time I could remember being polite for months, but she inhibited my rude tendencies the way Air-Wick inhibits onions.

I tried again. "About the anonymous letter," I said, "are you sure it isn't something for the police? Is it a threatening letter, or a blackmail attempt?"

"Neither. And it is not for the police."

"This is something out of my usual line of work."

She looked at my curiously. "What is your usual line, Russell? I haven't followed your career. I mentioned this business to Neville Markham and he told me you had done a very good job for him once. What kind of job would that be?"

"I don't suppose it's confidential," I said. "Someone in Markham's company was losing way too much money in the stock market. Markham naturally wondered where the money was coming from. It turned out the man had a wealthy aunt who'd just died, that was all. That's the type of job I do. I usually work for business firms, not for individuals. I call myself a private investigator but I'm really just offering service to business, like a corporation lawyer or a chartered accountant."

"But you are licensed as a private detective?"

"Private investigatory," I said, "yes."

"I imagine that means you can carry a gun," she said thoughtfully. "Yes, Russell, I believe you are the person I want. I should like to retain you. How much would that cost?"

I smiled. "I'm very professional about my rates," I said. "Would you ask a doctor how much he was going to charge you?"

"Of course."

"I bet you would, at that. Well, I charge like a doctor does. A little bit for how much of my time and professional training it takes. But mainly I charge for how much the job is worth to the party retaining me, and how much he can afford to pay."

"You're a good deal more frank than my doctors," she said. "I'll be satisfied with that. I'll give you a retainer of one thousand dollars, and you may let me know when I've had that much of your time."

"I still don't know what the job is."

"Open the top drawer of the desk," she told me. "The letter is there. You may read it."

The letter was on top of piles of neatly arranged

stationery. It was an ordinary business-size envelope, not cheap and not too expensive, stamped, postmarked Montreal two days before, addressed by typewriter to Mrs. Martha Scaley, 104 Belmont Terrace, Westmount. Inside was a single sheet of paper. I drew it out and unfolded it. A plain sheet of typewriter bond, Glasgow Bond, the watermark said; there was probably some in half the offices in the country. The message was brief, typed by someone who knew how to operate a mill, neatly set out on the paper and with the keys struck evenly. Probably a professional typist. You could develop the paper for latent fingerprints, but that wouldn't tell you who to look for unless the prints were on file. You could identify the typewriter used to write the letter, after you spent two years taking typing specimens from all the machines in the city. The message was unheaded and unsigned, and it said:

> Your daughter Inez' marriage is no good. John Sark was married before and never divorced, or if divorced it was not done in a way to leave him legally free to marry again in the Province of Quebec. I am not able to prove these statements but I am sure you will be able to do so on investigation. I advise you to get your daughter to leave Sark and obtain evidence for legal separation. This will save Inez a lot of grief.

I read it slowly, twice. I looked at Mrs. Scaley. She wasn't a nice old lady any more. She wasn't a cultured, peaceable, silver-haired old mother. She wasn't a mother at all. She was an old rich bitch, a frustrated autocrat, a woman who had been crossed but was going to have her way in the end after all.

I held myself back a little. All I said was, "I suppose

you didn't approve of this marriage in the first place."

"No, frankly, I didn't. But I didn't try to stop it. There were a lot of things I could have done that I did not do."

"But this proves you were right."

"I don't know what I was afraid of, exactly. I was afraid of something."

"And this is my job," I said. "All you want me to do is find John Sark's first wife. All you want me to do is break up your daughter's marriage."

"I think it's broken up already," she said. "I'll tell you about that. What do you know of John Sark?"

"Not much. The stories say he was born in Toronto and grew up there. In the twenties he ran liquor across the border. Across Lake Ontario, actually, because his headquarters was somewhere in Ontario. That's something against him, sure, but if you aren't born with money you have to make it somehow. He came to Montreal and went respectable. Ten years ago, maybe. He runs the Spadina Club, which is a respectable night spot, he's never been convicted of a crime or misdemeanour, he has a two-storey thirteen-room apartment in the building next to the block mine is in, on Cote des Neiges Road; he throws wonderful parties for Westmount people, and he married Inez six months ago."

"He runs the Spadina Club. Do you think that is all he does?"

"I know it isn't. I know he owns a couple of high-class gambling houses outside the city limits, I know he plays the dirty side of politics, and I've heard rumors of other activities. But I left that out because I'm not going to build up your side of the case. I'm with Inez. If she married him because she loved him, it's the most courageous thing a Scaley ever did, and I hope she's happy ever after."

The old lady's eyes were level, there was no doubt of that. She at least thought she was being honest. "Inez didn't love him," she said. "I think she married him from sheer boredom, because he was tougher than she was."

"You make her sound like a sweet kid."

"I've always loved her. I couldn't help what your money did to her. In days like these, when the government has taken over most social responsibility, wealth doesn't carry social obligation any more. It's wicked to be wealthy, in the eyes of the majority, and young rich people too often act as though they were trying to live up to that reputation."

"Let's leave the social philosophy out of it," I said rudely. "Let's keep it simple. Inez married someone you don't like. So you get this anonymous filth about Sark being a bigamist and you want me to find proof of it. You know what you should do with the letter? Burn it, and forget you ever saw it. Let Inez run her own life. She's a big girl now."

"It is not that simple. Sark has left Inez. Or at least, he has disappeared."

"She told you so, or someone else told you?"

I'd gone a little too far with that one, and she let me know it. "You seem to have a misconception of the relations between Inez and myself," she snapped. "I have not disowned her because I dislike her husband. We are as close and as cordial as we have always been. Inez moved back here with me five days ago. Her husband had disappeared without telling her anything. No one in the Spadina Club knew where he had gone. Inez was extremely angry. She came here and she has not tried to locate Sark since she left his apartment."

"After five days, that doesn't sound too serious to me. Maybe he was called away suddenly on business. Let's take a dim view and say perhaps he had to hide out from something for a day or two, and couldn't even call Inez. That could happen, in his line of work. He may be back in his apartment right now, too proud to call her. You said he's tougher than she is."

"There is more. Inez is through. A lot has happened since the wedding, six months ago. She wants to be rid of him. I won't tell you about this letter until I'm sure there is some truth in it, but it may be the best way out. Believe me, I am not in any sense trying to run Inez' life. I am trying to help her. And I need not ask you to believe me in all this. Go to Inez and tell her I have employed you to locate John Sark. Say I have reason to fear he met with an accident, or make up any story you wish. You will find out whether she wants him back."

"I'll take the case," I said. "On these terms: I tell Inez everything, and see what she wants me to do."

Martha Scaley frowned, changing from an ageless matron to a worried old woman. "No. It's too early for that. But you can do something just as good. If your investigation shows that Sark is still really encumbered with another wife, make your report to Inez instead of to me. Let her do just what she wants to about it."

I thought that over. "All right," I said finally. I stood up to go. "I won't thank you for the business. Into each life, and so on."

"When will you see Inez?"

"Where is she tonight?"

"Out with a party of friends."

"I'll probably find her," I said. "I'll go where a party of her friends would go."

Scene Two

NOTHING REALLY HELPS when it is August-hot in
Montreal, but a fast roadster is about as good as you can
get unless you want stale air-conditioning mixed with two
hours of Hollywood hashish. I drove around for about
an hour after I left Martha Scaley – out Decarie Boulevard
to the traffic circle and all the pretty new industrial plants
with landscaped grounds and show windows, then down
Cote de Liesse and slowly back into the city along the
narrow, winding old Lakeshore Drive. I cut up to Sherbrooke Street and came back to the hot center of town
and parked just past the Ritz. I picked my way through
the sidewalk café in front of the Trafalgar and turned left
into the bar. I sat down at a little table near the door, as
close as I could get to where the air-conditioning unit
exhaled its clammy breath. I'd stopped sweating, driving
the Riley, so no frost formed on me.

I sat and waited for Inez, because it was the best place
I could think of to wait and Inez would be there sometime
through the evening. I basked in the air-conditioning and
enjoyed the snow-rich taste of my drink, but I was bored.
Alan MacArnold came in. I was almost glad to see him.

MacArnold rode the police beat for the *Clarion*, the
local English morning paper. He wore unpressed grey
flannels and an elk's-tooth-patterned sports jacket and a
fedora that had been fished out of a storm sewer. He took
the fedora off in bars and private houses, and he had his
top collar button buttoned behind his tie, so he wasn't

quite a typical reporter. Not quite, but almost. He had the reporter alcohol appetite, the reporter world-weariness, and the cynical reporter social philosophy.

I nodded to him and he came and sat with me.

"I'm writing a story," he told me, "does this look like a good place to write a story?"

"Where does your editor think you are?"

"Out watching a corpse be tidied up, but he's been tidied up."

"Who got knocked off?"

"Nobody you know. Little lug with a lame leg that kept the accounts for the Spadina Club. His name was Sammy. Just Sammy. No more name than that, not that the cops could find, anyhow. It makes a fine story lead. 'Sammy was found dead last night. He was shot and he bled considerably.'"

"Who shot him?"

"The cops don't know, so how would I?"

"You might have an idea."

"I might."

I signalled and got another round of drinks. On my tab. The spirit moved Brother MacArnold to talk.

"It's all rumor, Russ. But the boys with the knowledge say Albert Geysek was sprung last week. Nobody can find Sark anywhere. And Sammy's been with Sark for a long, long time.

"Add it up," I said, "it's off my beat."

"You never heard of Albert Geysek?"

"I never heard of Albert Geysek."

"You know that Sark ran ram. I mean run rum. Hell. He ran hootch into New York state across Lake Ontario, back in the Volstead days. Albert Geysek was his partner. I'll bet Sammy worked for them. Why you never heard of

Geysek is, he got picked off his boat one night by a Yankee Patrol. He was making brooms for the U.S. government until sometime last week, when they kicked him off the free board list and gave him a one-way ticket back across the border."

"Geysek came back to Canada," MacArnold said, "and he came here to Montreal to get Sark. How do I know? Because, the wise apples say, the Sark crossed him when he got caught. There Geysek was, alone in the States with no dough and no friends. Unless Sark sent some money he couldn't even hire a lawyer. But Sark acted like he'd never heard of Geysek, after the guy was pulled in. Maybe it was the easy way to take over Geysek's half of the business. Anyway, the story says Geysek didn't forget. He had twenty years to think it all over. He wanted to have Sark's head on a plate. And he wanted Sammy too. That's my guess."

"What do the cops think?"

"They don't think. They don't know about Geysek getting sprung. They are inclined to suspect Sark because Sark is missing."

"How do you know he's missing?"

"That's how I know. Because the cops tried to locate him. And that is another thing that makes it sound less like a Sicilian fairy story. The Sark was scared crazy that Geysek would come here. For a year he's had two lugs that would be no use to anyone in the world except for bodyguards. As soon as he hears Geysek is loose, he hides out."

"Maybe," I said, "and then again, maybe he's hiding because he shot Sammy." But when I thought, I knew that wasn't true. Because I knew Sark had been hiding five days. This Geysek story could be the explanation.

MacArnold's glass was empty again, but I made no move to get it refilled. The bar was filling up and getting noisier. Any minute now Inez was going to come in, and I wanted her seat vacant and ready for her.

After a while he took the hint and moved on. After a while Inez came in, with a party of five or six. They sat down at the other end of the room, beside the high clean bar with the screwy mural on the wall behind it. I got hold of a waiter and told him to ask her over to my table.

"You know who she is, don't you?" he protested.

"I grew up with her. Skip."

"You know who she married?"

"I know who she married," I said. "This is strictly business. Skip."

Bob skipped. Inez came over after a few minutes. She was always a tomboy. She'd grown up to be a big, affectionate horse of a girl. She was at least five foot eleven, built perfectly to scale with wide hips, a rounded but firm belly and big high-hung breasts. That was the body. It was done up in the most striking quiet little summer dress that could be bought, given good taste and all the money in the world.

"Hi, Russ," she said, and flopped herself into the chair opposite me. "How are you, playmate? One of my friends a parolee you helped jail?"

I said, "Hi Inez. I hear your husband walked out."

"All Montreal's heard my husband walked out. You're just more tactful than most."

"Your mother told me. She wants me to find him. She thinks something's happened to him."

"She wishful-thinks something's happened to him. All right, go find him. Or find his body, I don't care. You get lower as time goes on, Russ. I haven't heard of you bringing together wife and missing mate before."

It seemed as if Martha was right. Maybe it was only temporary, but Inez was one hundred percent fed up with Sark just now. She'd be glad enough to have him tossed out of her life for good. Let her insult me if she wanted to. Coals of fire would be heaped.

"I have to have my office rent," I told her, "and I have an Indian rug I'm buying on time. So I'll find him for you." (And when I find him, I'll ask him something – something about John's other wife.) "How did he happen to leave? Anything unusual?"

"He just didn't come home one night. That wasn't too unusual. He often worked at the Spadina or one of his other places all night, then came home and slept in the daytime. This was last Friday. I was out all day. He still wasn't home when I got back. We were supposed to got out for dinner, so I called the Spadina. He'd left there at two a.m. Then I checked his clubs up north. He hadn't visited them. He's just vanished. I waited till Saturday night and then got mad and gave the servants a holiday and went home to mother."

"Since then?"

"Nothing. And I haven't asked."

"So maybe he checked back into the apartment."

"Maybe."

"Let's go look. I don't want to waste effort."

You could suggest anything to Inez that night. She was tired. She shrugged. "Why not?"

She went back to her party and got her handbag, and she spent twenty-three minutes in the women's while I smoked in the lobby, and then we went out and got into the roadster. Some cool air was trying to blow down on the city from Mount Royal but the hot breath of the sidewalks was pushing it back. We turned toward the cool air and went up Cote des Neiges to Westmount Boulevard.

The big apartment house everyone calls the Castle stands on the east or mountain side of Cote des Neiges, a great turreted tessellated greystone pile with a yawning hole in the center where you drive into park your car in the courtyard. Damp, cavernous corridors. The kind of place that has automatic elevators, but an operator to run them. But the operator was dumb and sleepy.

Inez was not looped, which I could tell only because I knew her. She was bored. Bored with life and with me and with John Sark, present, missing, or dead. She was a big girl, like Bergman, and she had the short curly blonde hair that Bergman had in Technicolor in *For Whom the Bell Tolls*, and the only real difference between her and Bergman was, Bergman was alive.

She fished a key from her plaid feed-bag purse and snick-snacked it in the door and we went in. The lights were all on in the apartment. We were both surprised.

"Somebody must be here," she said.

"Or has been here," I qualified.

The place was just like a house, except no snowy driveways, furnace stoking or garbage problem. It was a two-story apartment with four bedrooms upstairs and six rooms downstairs and enough rooms for servants and miscellaneous to bring the grand total to thirteen.

The entry was a big square room in black and white marble, two storys high, with a circular staircase straight ahead. It had a crystal chandelier as fancy as a young boy with dark red fingernails, and a floor of black and white marble squares big enough to play human chess on. Straight ahead where the staircase curved high was a corridor running the length of the apartment. Its light was also lit. But there was nobody in the corridor and no noise came from it. No noise came from anywhere.

"Hi, there! Who's home?" Inez called.

The chandelier tinkled a bit, laughing at us. Nobody answered.

I thought about Albert Geysek. I felt creepy as a man staked out on an anthill.

I hoped Sark had come back and Geysek had come here and killed him and nobody was here now but his body. I told myself Geysek wouldn't wait here for Sark to come in, not with all the lights on. I tried to make myself believe that. I didn't believe it a damned bit.

"Wait a minute," I told Inez.

I went down the bright corridor. It had dark red carpeting, some darker than dried blood but bloodstains wouldn't show too much. Every time I put a foot forward I chanted under my breath: Geysek, I am not the Sark; Geysek, I am not the Sark; just as though he could hear me. Maybe he could, I thought.

There were four doors, all on the right, as I went down the corridor. The doors were open and the rooms beyond them were black. Each time I went past one of those holes of danger my nerves went a little twangier. If someone had scratched a match I'd have dived into the ceiling up to my ankles.

There was a fifth door on the right, just at the end of the corridor. The door led into the kitchen, and the kitchen light was on. I looked in. I looked around for about a minute. Then I went back to Inez.

"Come on," I said, "we're going. In fact we were never here."

"Is anything wrong?"

"You left the frig door open," I said. "All the milk will be sour."

"Well, why didn't you close it?"

"Think of the things you can make with sour milk. Come on, will you?"

"Where?"

I snapped the button on the Yale so I could get back in and then I got her out the door. "Home," I said.

I made her walk down the eight flights to street level. I banked on how sleepy the elevator operator had been. I didn't think he even saw her going up. There was no doorman. We got into the roadster and got it out of the courtyard very quietly – no lights till we hit the street.

"What's the matter?" she asked me again.

"Nothing," I said. "Look, this is what you did. You left your party at the Trafalgar because you had a headache. You got into a cab about a block away from the Traf, because there wasn't one right at the door, and you went straight home. Straight to your mother's place, that is. Is there anything wrong with that?"

"No," she said without much enthusiasm. "Whom do I tell this to?"

"Anybody who asks."

We drove in silence for a while along the quiet Westmount streets. Then she said, "Tell me, has something happened to John?"

"I don't know," I lied.

A lot had happened to John, but I didn't tell her. It was better if she knew nothing about nothing. Besides, I didn't think she really cared.

Scene Three

AFTER I GOT BACK from the Scaley shanty and got rid of the car in its own garage it was one o'clock. My apartment was in the building next to Sark's. It just took minutes to get back to his place, and into that kitchen.

The kitchen was full of fat, modern white enamel gadgets streamlined enough to tow behind a jet plane without creating a drag. There were gadgets to heat, freeze, wash press, dry suck, spray grind, and open cans. There was nothing for delivering babies, but once you were born you could live your life there, with a telephone and a good set of delivery boys. You could do anything in that kitchen. You could even commit the perfect murder. Kill a man, wash the place and all your clothes with the appropriate gadgets, and dispose of the body without a trace. There was a garburator.

The murderer hadn't thought of that. He'd been old-fashioned, used a gun and beat it.

The floor was covered with dark blue linoleum. The big pool of blood beside the body was purple-black. A few minutes ago it had been growing as blood drained from the corpse, but now it was coagulating, hardening into a dark, scummed gelatinous mass. The stiff had been shot three times though the upper body, probably with a heavy-calibre gun because there was an awful lot of blood.

He had just opened the frig door, for a snack maybe or for a beer, when he got dead and fell on his face. The frig door was open and the beer was getting warm as the body got cool.

There were two things you could say about him for sure, besides that he was dead. First, it was John Sark, all right. His head was turned to the left and the deep-set haggard eyes, the Great Profile nose, the squared chin were Sark's. Second, he had nothing on but a sheet. He was wrapped in it. It was a fine, slick sheet and it was drawn tightly around his body, and it was clear he had nothing on underneath. Not so much as a pair of drawers.

There wasn't much I could do without leaving my spoor behind, so I went looking for a phone. There was one on a marble pedestal in the marble entry. It should have been a black marble telephone to match, but you can't have everything.

I got MacArnold's number from the book and dialed it with my pen. He let it ring seven times before he answered. He was two-thirds drunk and more than that asleep.

I said, "Teed here. Imagine I just slapped you twice on each cheek."

"And a merry Christmas to you, too," he told me and hung up. I dialed again. When he answered he said, "Look, I got a much better number you can call. Two redheads. Wait, I'll get it."

"You want the biggest exclusive since Louie Berkovitz gave himself up to the *Herald*?"

"Sure. Tomorrow."

"I'm at John Sark's apartment," I said meatily.

He bit on that. He chewed it over like a man eating his first oyster off the half-shell.

"Come on up," I suggested. "Get out of the taxi in front of the place. Make noise. Come on up in the elevator and ask the boy for Sark's apartment number. The door's unlocked. Come in and whistle."

He was sober. He was awake. He was excited. "Five minutes," he promised. He dropped his phone trying to hang up fast.

I took my handkerchief and wiped off Sark's phone and then I went upstairs. There was a long, carpeted corridor, just like downstairs. It was lit, like downstairs. This first room opening off it was also lit. The master bedroom. Thick, mushroom rug on the floor, the same kind I was taking two years to pay for. Furniture of wood grown in a cellar. Olive-green drapes and the thrown-back bedspread, crimson for contrast on the straight lamp shades, in the picture-frames on the wall.

An enormous bed. One sheet only. And the sheet had been slept on, or lain on.

The Sark's personal effects were spread out neatly on the bedside table. A pile of change, a package of Player's Mild and a gold cigarette lighter; a key case and a neat, thin black morocco wallet. And an old envelope, an old letter that had been carried around in his pocket for a long time. A window envelope with the address showing through from the bill inside: 'Mr. John Sark, 3975 Cote des Neiges Rd., Montreal.' I squeezed the envelope open and I could read the bill; it told him he owed the Dyker Caterer Service all of $150 for the month of July. That was neither surprising nor interesting. But below the window of the envelope, on the narrow strip of white paper there, something was drawn.

Just a line drawn along an old envelope. Straight, then diagonal, then straight, then diagonal again. With dots wherever the line changed direction, and something written beside each dot. Starting, going straight, then 'Pdmt.' Diagonally almost at right angles to the left, and then 'St.S.' Straight on again, and 'M.Hts.' Then diagonally to the right, ending with 'white rock', an arrow straight left, and at the end of the arrow a diamond drawn. In the middle of the diamond was the end of the trail – an X.

So that was that. And what's in the wallet?

I got it carefully by the edges, letting it swing open as I lifted it. No teedprints on this; I was doing it all with my fingernails. I had a celluloid insert holding Sark's driver's license, his membership cards in the St. Mathew Club and the Cote Skeet Club, and an old 1939 National Registration card. In the other side, a check for a watch left at Morton's, a tailor's bill for $160 from Gwyneth's on Beaver Hall Hill receipted for a $50 deposit, a business card presented by Roland S. Whitcomb of Cramer and Whitcomb, Members, Montreal Stock Exchange and Members, Montreal Curb Market, and a receipt for an old registered letter. In the money fold at the back of the wallet was a dun-colored hundred-dollar bill, another, a fifty, twenty, three ones, and a ragged piece of folded newsprint.

I sneaked the paper out gingerly and unfolded it. A smiling girl stared at me full-face. She looked familiar, but perhaps it was just the type that was familiar. Show-girl. Carefully blonde hair, probably ash-blonde or it wouldn't photograph so light, very long and straight and glamor-cut. Laughing eyes – how did those babes make their eyes laugh? Long nose, but all right in a rather long face. Curved open lips showing teeth that were retouched straight and gleaming. Bare shoulders. And it was torn off, above the caption, leaving no lead to who she was. But that could be found out. I folded the pic again, but I put it in my pocket instead of back in the wallet.

I put the wallet down, and there was nothing else in the room. Nothing else at all. Things were so neat. They were too neat.

The bedroom was furnished for one; Inez probably had her own room next door. Here in the Sark's chamber were a bureau with a big mirror, a high chest of drawers, nighttables on either side of the big bed, and two chairs, all in the same drab pale wood. The bed was turned down and mussed, the pile of junk from Sark's pockets was on the near bedside table, but beyond that there wasn't even an old sock lying around.

All right. Reconstruct. The Sark comes home tonight. Inez has been away five days so maybe he comes home before tonight, but if so he'd get the servants here in the daytime to tidy up, so that doesn't count. He comes in, gets undressed. He is very goddam neat, isn't he? He empties his pockets on the table and takes off his suit. He hangs up his suit. Okay, so would anybody. Then he takes of his shirt and hangs that up, and he takes off his drawers and hangs them up, and he takes off his shoes and socks and hangs them up. In a stoat's eye, he does. If they're not here, they're in a pile on the closet floor. But they weren't in the closet, because I looked. I put my handkerchief over the knob and opened the door. There was nothing in the closet but a neat row of shoes on the floor and a neat row of suits on hangers on the rail. And on a hook, a dressing gown. And on another hook, a laundry bag. And in the laundry bag, two-thirds of five-eighths of nothing at all.

I could have looked in the bureau drawers, but so few people put used shirts and drawers and socks back in bureau drawers. I could look in the bathroom. I did. There wasn't a laundry hamper in there, and there were no clothes lying around.

Where were we?

The Sark came home to go to bed. Emptied his pockets. Hung up his suit. Put his shoes on the closet floor.

Took of his shirt, socks and drawers and retired in the nude. With a sheet over him. Then he heard a noise in the kitchen, so he got up to investigate. He didn't go over to the closet and get his dressing gown and put it on. That was too easy. Any dope could do a thing like that. Sark was different. He pulled the top sheet off the bed, wrapped it around his bare buff, and went downstairs to be knocked off. You might think he knew he was going to need the sheet for a shroud.

MacArnold whistled. It was about time. I was getting nowhere. I was getting cold faster than the body.

He was standing on a black marble square in a double corner. I came down and stood on another black square and said, "Check. Mate in three moves."

"Go to hell. What gives?"

"I wouldn't know, I ain't here. You came here because you got information the Sark had returned. I don't know who told you. Maybe it was a newsie on St. Catherine. Maybe it was just a general rumor, and you can't remember who told you, yourself. You wanted to interview Sark about Sammy's death. You wanted to get his views on whether Geysek did it. Or did you? How should I know? I can't read your mind. Anyhow you came here. The door was open and you walked in. The lights were on, like they are now, and you went to the kitchen and guess what you found?"

"Guess what I found!" he yelped. He ran for the kitchen.

He got out there and stopped and looked. No matter how eager, it was something to stop and look at.

"God! How'd you happen to find him?"

"I didn't find him," I said patiently. "I've never found a corpse in my life, and I'm not going to start now. It's way out of my usual line of business. I don't want anything to do with the police. I have my reputation to think of. You found him."

"How about my reputation?"

"How about your exclusive?"

"John the Sark," he glommed, "shot in a sheet."

He began to get more excited. "Sark. Sark was shot in a sheet." He glared around. "Telephone?" he popped, and scampered.

I got there faster. I surrounded the telephone.

"Fingerprints!"

"Okay, fingerprints. I'll use my handkerchief."

He used his handkerchief. He dialed the *Clarion*. "Hi. Give me Hatch," he yapped. Pause. "Hay, Hatch! Can you tear out the second front on the Provincial?"

I could hear Hatch, the night editor, from three feet. He snarled, "The Provincial is in bed, and so are you. Hang up."

"Hatch, guess who got shot in a sheet?"

"*What* did you say?"

"Shot. In a sheet. John the Sark!"

Then he just stood there waiting, listening. Hatch wasn't even on the phone any more.

I walked away quietly.

I knew what Hatch was doing. I could almost hear him yelling. He was stopping presses and goosing photographers and hauling a rewrite joseph to the phone and composing a new front page for the second half of the Provincial.

I went out the door forever.

Scene Four

I COULDN'T SLEEP.

Maybe because of the heat. It was hotter than hell. It was hotter than a fundamentalist thinks hell is. It was hotter than it had ever been before anywhere else in the world. It was almost as hot as it had been in Montreal last August.

Who shot sheeted Sark?

It was a nice tongue twister. I said it again, out loud. It came out right the first time. So I wasn't going to sleep at all. Maybe it wasn't the heat. Maybe it was something I'd been trying to push to the back of my mind – a subconscious desire to drive up to the Laurentians.

I got up and got dressed and figured. I figured this way: Somebody shot the Sark in a sheet. You couldn't get away from that. Neither could Inez. The John Laws, *les Jean Lois*, were going to get very inquisitive with Inez. Scaley money or no Scaley money. Maybe she had an alibi. Maybe the alibi wasn't watertight, because unless you plan a murder you never have a watertight alibi. Hack but true, Russell, my boy. So she was involved. I was part of an alibi for her and if she used me *les Lois, Jean*, would begin to get very interested in me.

That made me have very good reasons for wanting to know who shot sheeted Sark. Several of them. So I was going to do the only thing about it I could do at this time of the morning. I just stopped for one drink first. And I just drank straight rye, because it was what I needed; I wasn't sleepy but I was tired.

Then I went downstairs and got the car and started up north. I went out Cote des Neiges, Queen Mary Road, and Decarie Boulevard. The night spots on Decarie's sunset strip were a glow of prism-reflected light ahead, then flashes of jittering neon – FDR's, Miss Montreal, Ruby Foo's – then a small disturbance in the rear view mirror. After that, the street lights of St. Laurent with the black houses being slept in, and then the straight broad silent road to St. Jerome.

I didn't have to slow much for St. Jerome, and I made fine time on the Laurentian Highway and from the turn-off at Piedmont through St. Sauveur to Morin Heights. Then the road I took was unpaved and twisting, sneaking through narrow passes between Laurentian hills and traversing up the steep sides of the ranges. A few minutes after we left Morin I found the white rock of the map.

Ahead the road angled to the right, avoiding a steep wooded bluff that went far up beyond the reach of the headlights. There was a bald spot on the almost vertical wall of the cliff. Somebody had painted a large white circle on the rock.

At the foot of the bluff a track, narrow and overhung by branches, led at right angles from the side of the road. I turned onto the track and let the Riley slow to a crawl. It was rough and rutted, skirting huge sitting boulders and bouncing into little gullies and out again. It took fifteen minutes to go two miles, and when the road abruptly ended dawn was breaking.

The track stopped at the edge of a lake, with a boat-house to the left and a parked car to the right, off the track and fairly well hidden in the brush.

The sun was coming up toward me as I faced the lake. There was no wind and the lake began to shine smoothly red and burning orange on the surface. The sky was lightening from midnight blue to azure, and the forest from midnight green to viridian. And the blessed sun had no heat in it. The sun was cooler than I could remember, having just lived through two weeks of August.

Just the relief of being out of the city was almost too much. I felt a little giddy. I couldn't believe the lake wouldn't start to bustle. I put both hands out in front of me, over all of it, to hold it still. I stopped feeling like a tired, hungover lug looking for a murderer. I felt more like a young faun looking for a dryad.

But I had to act like a lug. I went to the parked car sitting in the brush beside the track and went over it. It was a four-door closed job, three years old, maroon. It was shut up tight and locked. There was a car-rug lying bunched up on the right end of the front seat, as though someone had pulled it off the rack and then dropped it there. Nothing was on the back seat at all. The license tag was 53-633 and the mileage reading was 23,686. It had been well taken care of, and it hadn't stood outdoors many nights, but it looked as though it had been out all night this time; its windows were stippled with dew.

I left it and walked back toward the boathouse. I was just behind the Riley when I saw the dryad I'd been waiting for.

She was a water dryad, and she came dripping crystal sparks of light from the lake, and it was getting brighter, and than was very good.

She was tall and very brunette and there was no part of her that was not beautiful. No part, definitely. She was dressed in brief white nylon panties, very wet, very transparent. She had dark skin that she had tanned somewhere in private so it was all tanned, including the skin under the nylon. She wore no bra. She had probably never worn a bra. Her breasts were high and firm and pointed and she would need a bra as much as a drill sergeant would need a second backbone.

Her hair was long, black, heavy and plentiful. It was soaked but didn't straggle. It clung about a face that made me lift my eyes from her body. Long, even eyebrows, heavy-lidded eyes with the longest lashes in the world, straight nose and full lips. Her lower lip was more sensual than a Renaissance Venus. An archbishop would want to kiss that lower lip, would want to bite it until he drew blood.

She saw the Riley, and it surprised her. Her face didn't change expression but two dark little points of surprise pricked out on her. Then she saw me.

She looked me up and down, more in dismay than in anger. Then she took notice of the way I was looking at her, and the anger beat the dismay all hollow. "You," she said, "are trespassing." She said it in the tone used on men who wander into ladies' lavatories. "This is private property," she elaborated.

"Sorry. Somebody gave me this address and told me to ask for Clarence. You have to look all over to get a drink in this town before breakfast."

It wasn't funny. I didn't even think so myself.

She turned abruptly toward her car. In profile, the lower lip was irresistible. And she was still surprised.

She retrieved her car key from the only place she'd had to carry it safely, unlocked the car door, and reached for the robe. When she had wrapped herself as thoroughly as the bread wraps the ham in a railroad sandwich she turned to me.

"All right," she said, "turn that tin hot rod around

and get out of here."

"But I haven't had my swim yet."

"Look, Mister, I've got an X chalked on that rap, just where I'm going to ram it with my bumper. Move right now, or you'll be trying to pull the fender out of your tire for the next fifty miles."

"Let's start all over again," I pleaded. "I didn't see you come out of the lake. I didn't see you at all until you turned around with that robe draped over you. Heck, we can pretend, can't we?"

"All the fairy stories I know are Russian – and you know how they end. Will you please get the hell out?"

"I want to stick around for a while."

"This is just a private lake. There's nothing here at all. I don't know who you are or why you came, and if I wasn't here you could roam around the place all you wanted to. But I happen to own this lake, and I like it private. Please, go find another place to swim. You've got all morning."

"If you like it private, why'd you paint the white circle on the big rock by the highway?"

"So our friends could find the place. People we'd invited here. Know what I mean?"

"And you draw road maps for your friends, to show them which way to come?"

"No," she said flatly, "we don't provide that service, I'm sorry."

"You didn't draw a map for John Sark, for instance?"

"Who is John Sark?" she wanted to know.

"It doesn't matter," I said. I was tired. "It doesn't matter any more at all. I'll just look around for a few minutes, and then I'll go away and never come back. Not unless you invite me.

"I'll invite you," she said. "The weekend we're having my brother. The one who wears steel boots."

"Don't get mad," I said. I took a step toward her.

She didn't want me any closer. She jumped back into her car. I started over as she slammed the door. The idea was to lean on the window for a few friendly words, but she didn't want me near her. She started the engine. It took a minute for the motor to catch, as though the car hadn't been running for a while. She made a wide circle around the Riley and left, bouncing away along the track.

I took out my memo pad and wrote down her license number. I was glad I had that number. It might have something to do with Sark's death, and on the other hand it might not, but there were other reasons for writing it down. Three, including the lower lip.

Scene Five

AN X IN THE MIDDLE of a diamond; that was the way the treasure trail on the Sark's envelope ended. Supposing the diamond was the lake, the X might mean an island. And there the island was, not two hundred yards ahead. It was the only island on the lake. It was small and bald, with space for only one cottage on it. The cottage was a weather-beaten shack that had once been painted, with walls that had once been vertical and a roof that probably had not always sagged. It looked habitable, the way an open culvert looks habitable to a cold, wet, broke bindle-stiff. It didn't look like a place that would be owned by someone in Sark's social set.

Drawn up on the shore below the boathouse was a flat-bottomed punt, with oars pinned to its oarlocks. I shoved it off, caught two crabs with the left oar before I got the old technique back, and took a quarter-hour to get to the island.

The shack was even worse from close up. It was a dying place beginning to lose its sills and rot at the edges, all grown up in the raggedest of weeds and no path trodden to its door.

I pushed my way through burrs and matted tall grass to crooked steps that climbed the veranda. I ankled across the veranda, being careful where I put my weight, and tried the front door. It swung open.

The long front room ran from one side of the cottage to the other. A worn straw mat covered the floor. The walls were old unpainted wood, grey and hoary. At the left end of the room was a big trestle table with six wooden chairs around it. No three of the chairs matched. In the centre of the room opposite the door was an old cot with a patterned slip cover faded to several shades of dim rust, and two wicker chairs. At the right end of the room was a fireplace. There was an upholstered arm chair beside the fireplace. There was a man sitting in the chair. There was a large black hole in the centre of his forehead.

The man with the hole in his head was John Sark.

Someone had got to a hell of a lot of trouble just for me. They had stolen Sark's body from a slab in the morgue, trucked it fifty miles out of Montreal, set it in this chair and shot it through the head. Just so I could find it here. A hell of a lot of trouble. They really needn't have bothered.

But that was what they had done, because it was John Sark. He had been shot twice; once through the neck, and that had bled a lot. The front of him was mostly blood, soaking his shirt and tie and jacket. But the face was all right. It wasn't handsome, with that black hole in the forehead; too bad, because Sark had been a lady-killer when he was warmer and had all his blood in his veins. There had been a distinguished breadth to his forehead, a square forthrightness to his chin. His eyes had been deep set and understanding, his nose sensitively flaring, his lips heavy but firm.

The face was unmistakably John Sark. Just as unmistakably as the face of the corpse in the Cote des Neiges kitchen.

If somebody was playing games with me, they were damned silly games. I had seen enough of the corpse of Sark earlier in the evening. Enough corpse and enough blood to last me until the next war. I didn't want to play any more.

Just to be really sure, I got an unsoaked corner of the jacket and eased it away from his chest. I pulled his white shirt up out of the pants, and looked. No bullet holes in this chest.

Teed is crazy, or there were two Sarks.

Teed is crazy. No, no.

I got my hand under the waistband of the pants and dug until I came up with the top of a pair of violent yellow pure silk shorts. So much for drawers. I wasn't entirely crazy. At least this corpse had drawers.

I went all over the cottage. There was only the one floor. There were three doors opening off the main room. The first gave me a kitchen, a pump over an old tin sink, a wood stove, racks with piles of cheap china, no food. The second and third gave me bedrooms, and there was a back bedroom opening off one of these. The three bedrooms were pretty much alike. They were bare and rough-walled and wooden-floored, and they had chairs and tables and beds and mattresses and bent wire coat hangers and old toothpaste tubes that could have belonged to anyone. There were some books tucked up on shelves but nobody had thought enough of them to write a name on the flyleaf. They were mostly Edgar Rice Burroughs and Zane Grey so I was more annoyed than surprised at that.

In the back bedroom, tucked under the rim of the wash basin, was an empty bottle. The label said, 'One teaspoonful after meals, as required.' It came from Herbinger's Pharmacy, 4055 Cote Ste. Catherine Road, Montreal.

That wasn't much. But it was all. Except that in the back bedroom a blanket had been pulled off the bed and thrown back on it, in a heap.

I returned to the front room and looked at the corpse again. While I looked at him I remembered I hadn't eaten for twelve hours, but I only remembered because I was thinking I didn't want to eat again, not for a long time.

Scene Six

WHEN I GOT TO MY APARTMENT it was about seven-thirty. It was as hot as it had been yesterday, and the day before that, and the August before that, all in Montreal. I opened every window and fixed the fan to pull air from Mount Royal through the apartment. I took off most of my clothes, got a pint of beer from the kitchen, and then dialled the copes. I asked for Homicide, and I got Framboise.

"*Allo, allo,*" he said, "Framboise *ici.*"

"Hello. This is Russel Teed speaking. You've met me twice, Raoul. Once when you got me in to identify Karl Malan's body. Once when we met in that tavern on St. Peter and got drunk."

"Sure," Framboise said. He sounded very tired. "I remember."

"You been up all night?"

"*Oui.* I'm just going 'ome to bed."

"I've been up all night too."

"*Merci,*" he said coldly, "t'ank you for telling me."

"I found a corpse," I said. "I thought you might like to know. I came home to call you. He didn't have a phone."

Framboise grunted. "Give me details," he said. "A day sergeant will be here before eight and 'e will take it."

"No," I said. "You better take it. It was a body you'd be interested in. It was John Sark, and I found him five miles north of Morin Heights, about five-fifteen."

"*Seigneur! Vous vous êtes trompé,*" he snapped. "John

Sark, he was shot 'ere in Mo'real at one of this morning. We 'ave his body, all tagged and filed away in a drawer. You are crazy."

"I thought so myself," I admitted, "but I'm not *trompé*. I was never less mistaken in my life. I heard about you finding Sark. But I found Sark, too. Come on around I want to tell you all about it."

"Let us get t'is clear. You foun' a body? Regardless who it was, it was a body?"

"That's right," I said, "up north."

"Out of the jurisdiction of t'is department," Framboise said happily. "Wait. I get you the Provincial Police number."

I began to get mad. I was being a good boy and reporting a corpse. It wasn't very healthy for me to report this corpse. It might tie me in with the first body. It might even tie me into a murder charge. It might get Inez tangled with the law. But I had to get Framboise interested because otherwise God alone knew when anyone would find the body on the island. And I had to have it found. I needed help.

"Look," I said. "When you found Sark's body you went over his apartment. Of course. Did you see an old envelope with something drawn on it? It was in his bedroom."

"Yes."

"Did you figure out it was a road map?"

"*Oui, certainement*," he said impatiently.

"Well, I followed it. Right to the *X* in the diamond at the end. And that's where I found the second body."

That stopped him. He said resignedly, "W'ere are you?"

"Cote des Neiges, 3945. Top floor."

"Hokay," he said. "I'll get aut'ority to send some boys

up, for to collec' your body. T'en I will come see you."

He hung up. I hung up. The phone rang.

"Teed," I said, because this time of the morning it would have to be business.

It was MacArnold. "Have you seen the *Clarion*? We got a beautiful spread on Sark. Thanks, boy. Any time I can find another body for you —"

"I thought you'd be asleep," I said.

"I'm home now. Just turning in. I wanted to call you."

"Get dressed again. I'm at my place. The apartment number is 46, tenth floor."

"Now, wait a minute. I haven't been asleep since Monday."

"Neither have I. And I've found another body."

He said he'd be with me in another ten minutes.

I got another pint of Dow from the kitchen and went into the bedroom and lay down on the bed. I put the bottle in my mouth and let it rest on my bare chest. I took my hands away and let them flop. When I wanted beer to trickle down my gullet, I just arched my back.

My doorbell rang. The pint of beer rolled off my chest and gurgled into the mattress. I retrieved the bottle but it was half-empty.

I went to the door and opened it a crack, because I was in my shorts. It was MacArnold. He was a nice shade of dove grey, darkening to dull black below the eyes. I let him in. I left the catch off the door so I wouldn't have to get up again, and we went into the kitchen and got more Dow, and then came back to the front room and sat.

"I need a new story," I told him. "I have to have a story to tell Framboise. I can think of a couple. They aren't much good. Maybe you and I got talking in the Trafalgar, and I got curious about the Sark case and came to his apartment with you and we found the body. You let me leave before you called Framboise, because I wanted to stay out of it. That's one story."

"You're right," MacArnold informed me, "it isn't much good. For one thing, it makes me too big a liar."

"Then I'll have to use the other story. Play along."

"Okay, if I can. Spin it."

Just then the doorbell rang again. I yelled, "Come in."

Framboise was detective-sergeant in charge of the Homicide night squad. Framboise is French for raspberry, but he didn't look like a raspberry. Keeping it horticultural, he looked more like a raw potato: pasty, but hard. He had arms and legs built for a seven-foot man and a trunk built for a five-footer. He averaged out at six feet, a little grotesque but not awkward. He wasn't dumb. He spoke English with a considerable accent.

"Hi," I said. "MacArnold called me just after you hung up, so I told him to come around. Have a chair. Beer?"

He nodded, "*Merci.*" He sat down. I got up bandy-legged and went to the kitchen for more beer. The Dow pints were getting low, but there were quarts of Molson on the lower shelf. I opened two. Then I stood and listened for a minute. The kitchen door had swung to behind me, and they weren't talking in loud voices, but the acoustics were just right for listening.

"Who is t'is guy Teed?" Framboise asked softly.

"A private operative," MacArnold told him. "Very big-time. All kinds of contracts. Does mostly company work. Not the cases where the bookkeeper skips with a thousand iron men, the cases where the chairman of the board thinks the secretary-treasurer has been cooking the company balance sheet to buy himself a small republic in South America."

"He don' look the type," Framboise protested. "He don' look tough. He's thin enough to dissolve in a heavy rain. An' he does not move quickly."

"He's tired. Maybe he's thin, but he's got more sinew than a cheap steak. He's got a face that everybody loves and animals trust. And brains like an accounting machine."

That would do for the present. I came in with the beer.

"So you 'ave another body," Framboise said.

"Yes," I admitted. I poured him some beer. "I owe you an explanation. So does MacArnold. He didn't tell you the whole truth. When he found the body in the kitchen last night, he called me right away and I came to see it."

"You could lose your job for t'at," Framboise told MacArnold. "So easy, you could lose your job. An' get in jail too."

"It wasn't his fault. We were talking earlier in the evening, before he decided to go call on the Sark. He told me he thought Sark might get killed. I was working on a case that involved Sark, so I asked him to phone me if anything happened. Just as a favor."

"You were working on w'at?"

"No connection," I said, "I couldn't tell you if I wanted, but it has no bearing. Sark was just incidental in my case. But I was curious about him. I came over. I didn't go near the body, but I looked at the apartment. I saw the map. Later on I couldn't sleep, so just for the hell of it I followed that map. There was another corpse at the end of it."

"W'en was this?"

"About five-fifteen. The X in the diamond at the end of the map is an island in a little lake up north. There's a cottage on the island, and this body was sitting in the front room with a hole in his head. A big hole, maybe from a .45, that hadn't bled much, and another hole in his neck that had. He was pretty cold and stiff, so he'd been dead a while."

"I got aut'ority to go pick 'im up," Framboise told me. "How does the basket-wagon get t'ere?"

I told him how I'd got to the lake. There should be a scow drawn up on the shore there. They can row over to the island."

"A hell of a place to get a corpse out of," he grumbled. He wanted to telephone and I led him out to the entry. He called his office and talked for a while in French. I got another quart of beer and split it between MacArnold's glass and mine. The well was going to run dry if they stayed much longer.

When Framboise came back he said, "Hokay, now we come to the screwy part. T'is body, you say, was John Sark."

MacArnold choked on some beer he was drinking. He took out a handkerchief and wiped off his nose and lips.

I said, "Either it was the Sark, or there were two Sarks. They looked enough alike to be Siamese twins. If the one I found was just a cheap imitation, the one MacArnold found was genuine. Or maybe it was the other way around. Maybe the corpse in the kitchen was an imposter. Maybe he was just pretending to be the Sark."

"Nope," MacArnold said definitely. "I know Sark. That was Sark, the one I found."

"Wait till you see the second one. You won't be so goddamned sure. You'll think you're going crazy, like I did. I couldn't tell which one of them was the real article, and I'll bet I saw him alive as often as you did."

"It was still the Sark I found." MacArnold said obstinately.

"How the hell are you so certain? How does anybody know? The Sark was never convicted of anything. He was never printed. Put these two bodies side by side and the only difference between them will be the position of the bullet holes."

"I still say —" MacArnold began.

"Uh-huh. Were there ever any rumors floating around that Sark had a double?" I looked at MacArnold.

"No," MacArnold said. "Why would he want a double?"

"You know why. You told me about it yourself. You said Sark was scared to death. Geysek would get him. He'd had bodyguards for a couple of years. When he heard Geysek was out of the stir he was so frightened he disappeared. That all adds up to a man who would go to a hell of a lot of trouble and expense to protect himself. Say he found a guy somewhere who looked exactly like him — or say he found a lug who looked enough like him that a bit of plastic surgery would make them twins. There are doctors around who take on jobs like that.

"Somehow he gets a double. He keeps him hidden out under lock and key. His idea is, when Geysek is let loose the double will take over for him and stick around Montreal — while Sark hides out — until Geysek pops him. This is all a little fantastic. So is the idea of two Sarks, but I saw two Sarks."

"You say," MacArnold interrupted sceptically.

I ignored him and went on, "It adds like five and five, because if Geysek pops the double and gets fingered for it, the Sark is safe from then on. If he doesn't get fingered right away, he has to travel a long distance and take up residence in some underdeveloped country. Sark wins any way at all." I stopped for a slug of beer, and to find a cigarette.

"Take another thing, just a small point," I said. "Sark skips and goes somewhere to a hideout, but the double doesn't take his place right away. For five days there's no Sark, genuine or counterfeit, in the city. Sark's wife hasn't been told anything, so she gets mad and moves out of his apartment. Probably he knew her well enough to know she's likely to do just that. Then the double comes in and takes over with no awkwardness."

"No," Framboise said. "W'y not? *Sacré*, because the body in the apartment was the Sark. His wife identifies him. T'ey cannot look that much alike."

"Tell me one thing," I went on, "and I don't care which is which. Why did they *both* get killed? Let's assume the idea was that Geysek should shoot the double. Did he shoot both? Or did he shoot the double, and somebody else shoot Sark? No, no, there we go again. We can't tell why Sark was shot if we don't know which one was Sark."

"But we do know which one was Sark," MacArnold said passionately. I didn't pay any attention to him.

"And that isn't the only screwy thing about it. Take the corpse in the kitchen. The corpse in white. Framboise, did you ever see a corpse wrapped in a sheet before?"

He shook his head. "No. It's a funny one. I see t'em every way. Full evening dress, right down to nude. Once, even, a pair nude. One bullet t'rough both. They ..."

"Yeah, sure, I can imagine," I said. "But no sheets?"

"No sheets, no."

"How do you figure it?"

"He 'ad been sleeping, or anyway he lay down on the

bed. Nude, because of the heat. He hear' a noise in the kitchen, an' so he got up, he grabbed a sheet from the bed to wrap aroun' him, he came downstairs."

"And all the time his dressing gown is hanging on a hook in the closet right beside him."

Framboise shrugged. "People do crazy t'ings. W'at would you do if you t'ought it was a burglar you heard, in your kitchen? Would you go get a dressing gown? Maybe.. Maybe not. I don't know, me, what I would do."

"What would you do, MacArnold?"

"I don't have a dressing gown," MacArnold said. "Also, I don't sleep nude. In hot weather I sleep in my shorts. So I wouldn't wait to pull a sheet off my bed. I'd just get up."

"That brings us to another point," I said brightly. "And it raises the question, how screwy can things get? Because where were his shorts? His drawers? Some men don't have dressing gowns, or if they have them they don't use them. Some men also don't wear undershirts. I don't. But everybody wears drawers. Where were his drawers?"

"*Sacrement*," Framboise cursed, "w'at drawers?"

"He wasn't wearing drawers, was he?"

"No. He was wearing a sheet. Not'ing but a sheet."

"When he got undressed upstairs, he emptied his pockets. He left the things from his pockets on the table. But he didn't leave any clothes lying around. None at all. I looked. His suit he could hang up, and his shoes he could put in the closet. But you've got at least three things left: shirt, socks, and drawers. Where were they?"

Framboise got very red. "*Maudit cadavre*. I didn' t'ink of that."

"Maybe he put them in the laundry," I suggested.

Framboise brightened.

"I thought maybe he did. So I checked. He didn't."

That made him mad. "They mus' be somewhere," he said, a little excited. "I go back t'ere and look."

"The beer's all gone, anyway," I told him.

Scene Seven

I woke up slowly. I was bathed in sweat, the sheet damp and sticky beneath me. I looked at my watch and it was 3.15.

I was so hot, if I spit on myself it would sizzle.

I got up slowly, shoved damp hair out of my eyes, and looked fro bedroom slippers. They weren't there. The hell with bedroom slippers. Standing up very casually so my body fluids wouldn't get wrought up and boil away, I opened my eyes a little bit and felt my way to the kitchen. I got the last stubby pint of Dow from the refrigerator, poured all the beer neatly into a pint glass without raising any head, and drank deeply.

It came to me suddenly that just as I went to sleep I'd remembered something I'd forgotten, and now I'd forgotten again what it was. Men go crazy that way.

I concentrated very hard on not thinking about it, so I would remember. I concentrated on beer. Would I call up the grocery and order beer and wait for it to come, or would I just go out and get a drink somewhere? I went to the cabinet under the sink to see how many emptied I had, and I stubbed my toe on the cabinet door badly enough to take off some skin. I got mad and kicked the door and that took off more skin. By that time I was agitated enough to forget I was trying to think of something, so I remembered it. I went to the entry, found Framboise in the phone book, and called him.

Madame Framboise answered. She told me in French

that Raoul had just gotten up and was taking a bath, but then I heard him call to her that he was coming. "*Allo, allo,*" he said.

"It's Teed. I forgot something about the corpse in the kitchen. What about ties? I didn't see ties anywhere."

He was still sleepy, and that didn't mean anything to him.

"Ties?" he asked, puzzled.

"Cravats."

"Ho, *des cravats.* All his cravats were rolled up neat in 'is top bureau drawer."

"Well, that's that. How do you figure the thing?"

"He's lying in front of an open fritch door. So 'e's jus' going to 'ave something to eat or drink, *correct?*"

"Sure."

"We t'ink he's heard a noise in the kitchen, so 'e comes down to investigate. There is a big clothes-dryer machine in the kitchen, to the lef' as you come in, an' between the dryer and the far wall plenty of space for a man to crouch down an' hid. So the murderer, w'en he hears someone coming, crouches down, Sark comes in an' turns on the light. He sees not'ing suspicious. Now he is here he can just as well eat some food, or perhaps have a beer. He goes to the fritch an' opens the door. His back is to the murderer but 'e is between the murderer an' the way out. I t'ink he runs away."

"You mean, you don't think the murderer came there for the purpose of shooting the Sark? Why'd he come?"

"He was jus' a sneak t'ief. *Un voleur.* That is the way it looks."

"Yeah? A burglar plugging the Sark just by chance is likely as a test pilot dying in bed."

"It looks like a burglar."

"It was meant to look like a burglar."

"Hokay, I am dumb. I t'ink it is a burglar, like it looks, until t'ere is some evidence to make it look different."

"How about this big theory of MacArnold's? I suppose he told you. Albert Geysekf got out of jail in the States, came to Montreal, shot Sammy and they went gunning for the Sark. Doesn't that sound pretty good?"

"T'ere is not'ing to back it up, excep' we know Geysek was released from prison. Anybody could 'ave killed Sammy. He was all alone in his room on Ontario Street. Somebody shot 'im an' just walked away. Nobody in the house saw a t'ing. If Sammy had a caller, they didn't know. T'ey heard the shot, jus' after nine o'clock, and w'en they opened his door, t'ere he lay. Likely we will never 'ang it on anyone. Anybody could 'ave killed him. An' a *voleur* could 'ave killed Sark. We don' even know Geysek is in the city."

"You and your *voleur*," I grumbled. "The man who killed Sark or who killed the corpse in the apartment, I mean – how did he get into Sark's place?"

"The back door was locked and had a chain on it. Likely 'e went in the front. Maybe wit' a skeleton key. Maybe the door was open. It was open w'en MacArnold went in."

But not when I went it. So it was a skeleton.

"Did you find anyone who heard the shots?"

"No," Framboise said disgustedly. "The whole hapartment 'ouse, they were asleep or they were out.

I got dressed and got the Riley and drove down to Dorchester Street.

Louie Two's didn't open till five or whenever Louie Two woke up, but the door was never locked. The cash was cleaned out and the hard liquor was behind bars but the beer cooler was usually open. I went down the center aisle of the bar room between the tables, around the corner of the bar and through the swinging door. It was very dark. I was very thirsty. I got two quarts of beer from the cooler, hoping they were Dow; I couldn't read the labels. I tore what was probably a black page from my notebook, scrawled 'I.O.U. $1, Russ,' rang up No Sale on the cash register and dropped the slip in the drawer. Money was no good. A newsman might get to it before Louie Two woke up.

I got a glass and brought the two quarts back through the swinging doors to the barroom and sat down at the first table. It was very very dark. I could think better in the dark. I poured a beer and tasted it; it wasn't Dow. It wasn't Molson's, either. Even if it wasn't Dow or Molson's I could think better in the dark.

So far there were two dead men and three live women. Sark I and Sark II, Inez, the dryad at the lake, and the blonde in Sark's wallet. Two unknown women, to get found. And yet another: the woman who got me into the whole mess, Sark's first wife. Was she the dryad, the show-girl blonde, or was she a fourth femme?

When I'd investigated all these I could look for Albert Geysek and try to find out if he was in Montreal, but I was going to concentrate on the women first.

Starting to figure from the beginning, it was easy to go a little distance. The Sark had a double, that was doubtless. All well-organized dictators have doubles, and who was the Sark to let a dictator outdo him?

So there was Sark, and there was his double, and they both got shot. Which was which? By now I was pretty sure I had that one taped, so it didn't stop me. I went on. I went no further at all. Because why were they both shot?

Theory one, somebody meant to shoot Sark. Shot the double instead. Realized his mistake and proceeded to find Sark and shoot him too. Okay. So much for the theory one. Could be Geysek.

Theory two, somebody had planned to shoot the Sark and had shot the corpse in the kitchen. That could be Geysek again. Another party knew about the hide-out, where Sark was expected to be holed up, and went there to shoot the Sark, and shot the body on the island. So much for theory two. Theory two meant there wasn't much more than coincidence linking the two killings.

Theory three.... Was there a theory three? Sure. There was one other way it could be figured. And the more I explored it the more convinced I was it was the right way. It explained the puzzlers. It explained why the corpse in the kitchen was wrapped in a sheet, and why he had no drawers and no socks and no shirt. Sure, it was right.

It took longer than I realized to get this far, because the two quarts of beer were gone. I felt I must be up and doing. I up and did. I got into the Riley and drove down the hill to the *Clarion* Building, a dull, heavy pile of smoke-black stone, on Craig Street near the C.N.R. right of-way.

I've spent so much time at the *Clarion* on some of my cases, the elevator operator thinks I work here. He knows my first name. "Hi, Russ," he said.

"Hi, Dad," I cracked back. Scintillating repartee. A gallon of beer on an empty stomach and everything scintillates. I got off the elevator at the third floor and went to the library.

The librarian was the ugliest girl in Canada and she knew everything about everyone who'd been born and all the things that had happened to them since Columbus made his first landfall.

"Hi, Cassie," I said.

"Why, Russell! How are you!"

"Oh, just fine," I said. I thought of three minor league gags I could spout just to keep my reputation green, but it didn't seem worth the trouble. "I'm looking for a blonde."

"Wait, I'll go get my peroxide bottle."

"Ha-ha," I said, very politely. "You card, Cassie. This blonde I want, you had her in the paper. At least I think you did. All I have is a pic with no caption. The typeface on the back looks like the *Clarion*. Publicity still, probably on the amusements page. The newsprint isn't yellow, so it was likely within the last three months."

"Full-length, or head and shoulders?"

I dug in my pocket. I pulled out the torn scrap. "I've got it right here. Head and shoulders, full face. And nothing on the shoulders except the hair that grew that far down. Glamor-cut."

I began unfolding the pic but she didn't want to see it. "Sure," she said without hesitation. "I remember. Her name was Carol something. She is opening at the Caliban Club. I'll find it."

It was in the *Clarion* for June 18, and just the way Cassie remembered, it was headed 'Opening at the Caliban Club' and the cutline said, 'Carol Weller, mistress of terpsichorean perfection, will appear in the great Broadway Gaieties Review at the Caliban Club opening this Friday. Miss Weller has just completed a successful run at the Modine Hotel in Hollywood, and previous to that engagement had been a featured performer in numerous spots on the Great White Way.'

I looked again into the innocent, smiling eyes that had been folded into the Sark's wallet. So her name was

Carol Weller. So she danced. At the Caliban Club, yet.

The Caliban was as low you could get in Montreal. It was lower than the lowest of the English clubs, of the French clubs, of the Negro clubs. It was the lowest of the miscellaneous clubs, which started low and ranged on down through queers' meeting houses and quasi-circuses and spots where the girls would beat you up if you didn't take them home with you. And then we had the Caliban. If a man was found rolled and slugged and half-dead in the gutter, the first thing the cops did was put everybody connected with the Caliban on the griddle. Most of the time that turned up the mugger, or a lead to him. Then the Caliban got closed, and after a while it opened again.

How the girl got a publicity still into the *Clarion* when she was dancing and the Caliban was a good question, but mistakes are sometimes made at press time when material is thin. Also, the oddest characters sometimes get to buy beers for newsmen. Anyway there she was.

That took me to the Caliban. It was between St. Kits and Dorchester on a side street just west of Peel. It was also locked up tight, front and back.

I got the owner's name off the liquor license notice hung inside the glass of the front door. I called him, and he was out, and his wife said the place should be open but if it wasn't I was likely to find the manager drinking beer in the nearest tavern.

I went to the nearest tavern.

The Caliban's manager was recognizable because he wore a fifty dollar Panama and pure silk tie that had been painted either by Picasso or Vlaminck. He was sitting alone at a table sipping lager, and I joined him.

"I'm looking for Carol Weller," I said.

The Panama turned toward me. Under its brim were

a pair of black, hairy John L. Lewis eyebrows, the eyes and snout of an overfed pork, and a mouthful of black teeth. Deep purple lips drew back from the teeth. They looked as though they might crack in a brighter light. He said, "Okay, flatfoot. Look for her."

I got out a battered press pass I had printed up years ago and showed it to him. "I want to do a story on her."

The Panama regarded me listlessly. "You, newsman? Since when does a news guy want to do a story on a floozie that danced in the Caliban, Mac? Try again. Maybe you ain't one of the boys in blue, but you ain't from a newspaper. The last three collectors I seen had passes like that. One thing, I ain't responsible for her debts."

"Is she still dancing at the Caliban?"

"Nah. I threw her to the wolves after a week."

"What's her home address?"

"How would I know?"

"Okay, what was her phone number, then? You'd have that."

"What's it worth?"

"Ten iron men," I said, "and that's all."

The Panama thrust out a dark, greasy hand, palm up.

I said, "Yeah, and that number was?"

"Hell for ten bucks I'll give you her address. Come on over to the office."

We went, and he gave it to me, and it was worth a ten.

It was a good address, a few blocks away and a whole world apart from the Caliban. It was across St. Catherine and above Sherbrooke, on the mountain side, which made the magical difference. It was an old brick house on Peel, made over into apartments. The mail box labelled Carol Weller was No. 5, and the apartment labelled No. 5 took up about half of the second floor.

The girl in the picture came to the door when I rang. Carol Weller. She was wearing a baby blue negligee, clinging but not transparent. She might have had something on under it and she might not, depending on whether she was naturally endowed or went to a good corset-smith.

Her long blonde hair touched the collar of the negligée with its turned-up ends. Her face was frank and open as an empty wallet. The eyes were baby blue to match the negligee. They were neutral, inquiring. "Yes?" she asked. Huskily.

"Miss Weller?" I put on my best smile, and took off my best hat. "I'm a private investigator, working on a case. Could I talk to you for a few minutes?"

The eyes clouded over. They showed suspicion. I was quite sure it was because she wanted them to show suspicion. She had been laughing with the eyes, in the *Clarion* picture that found its way into the Sark's wallet. With the eyes only.

I tried a little harder. "This is a very serious case I'm on, Miss Weller. Two murders have been committed, maybe three. I think you're involved – not with the killings, of course, but with the case. The police haven't connected you with it yet. If we had a little talk, maybe they won't."

Everybody is a sucker for a dollop of blackmail.

"The police can investigate me if they want to," she said with dignity, from somewhere in her diaphragm. "I haven't anything to hide. Do you have a badge, Mr. –?"

"Teed. I don't carry a badge. Here's my card."

I got out one of the plain ones that said 'Russell Teed' and then in small print below, 'Investigations.' Not even a phone number. It's my Westmount card. I thought she might be impressed by class. "The name is Teed," I said.

"All right, Mr. Teed," she breathed. She turned and went back into the apartment, leaving me to close the door and follow.

The entry was done in jet and chalk-white and crimson, with much mirror. It let into a living room done with olive-green walls, a foam green rug as thick as underbrush along the upper Amazon, mahogany tables in ingenious, incongruous modern designs, and sectional furniture arranged in one of the 3,656 ways you can arrange a set of sectional furniture. It looked just beautiful. It looked like a $10,000 cheque to an interior decorator.

I sat down in a piece of sectional that looked less uncomfortable than the others. I put my hat back on, because I was going to act tough if I had to, and I would have to. In respect to that $10,000 I pushed the hat back on my head.

She looked at me steadily and said, "All right, give. What's it all about?"

She had arranged herself on another piece of the sectional, a piece with a back and one arm. She had thrown her elbows back and up to the top of these supports, to tighten and raise the line of her breasts. She was ready for anything. Only the sheerness of the negligée spoiled the effect, outlining a brassiere clearly. The bra was a crafty piece of heavy engineering.

"I suppose you know John Sark is dead," I said.

"It was all over the *Clarion* this morning. Some torpedo shot him in his own kitchen."

"Not only is the Sark dead. His double has also been operated on with a .45. Very messy."

"Well," she said, "well, well, won't that make a sensation. Who would have guessed the Sark had a double?"

"I thought you'd know," I said.

She took that with a smile, but the eyes got colder. "Spell out your goddamned insinuations," she said delicately.

"I thought you'd know he had a double, on account of your knowing the Sark so well."

The expression in her eyes changed. It was now earnest. Very earnest. She leaned toward me. "I didn't know him," she breathed. "I never even met him."

"Okay, then why was your picture found in his wallet when he was killed?"

"No!" she said in a pitiful little moan. The crimson lips trembled and the eyes were pained.

"Like I said, Miss Weller, he tore your pic out of the paper. He put it in his wallet. Right with his money. Why?"

"So my picture was in his wallet? What does that mean? Maybe he looked at it and had an idea he could use me in his Spadina Club. Maybe he liked my looks and meant to get in touch with me, for an audition. But he didn't. I never heard from him at all."

"Sure. Or maybe he sat at a ringside table in the Caliban one night and fell in love with you. Maybe he carried the picture around from pure sentiment. The pure holy sentiment of love."

"You're so bright," she said. "You're a little silver dream. I bet all the girls call you smiley."

"You're bright yourself," I said. "You're real beautiful for so early in the afternoon. Mother told me chorus girls were awful ugly when they got up in the afternoon."

"Watch the chorus girl routine, smiley. I'm a dance act," she said sharply. But the eyes were still earnest. She had wonderful control over those eyes.

"All right, so there's no connection between you and

Sark. They picture doesn't mean a damn thing. I'll give it to the police and admit I stole it from Sark's wallet. It won't matter."

She crossed her legs. The legs were beautiful and white and firm, without too much muscle. She wasn't wearing a slip, that much was clear. "You wouldn't do that," she said winningly. "It might get you into trouble. Why don't you just tear it up and forget it?"

"For a price."

"I can pay a price." She shoved her body at me.

"Information. What were you to him, Baby?"

She flipped a cigarette ash at a great heavy chunk of cut-glass ash tray — and missed. "All right," she said in a voice full of world-weariness. "I suppose you'd find out in the end anyhow. I knew him ten years ago. I was going to marry him."

I watched the cigarette ash. It skittered across the polished top of the dark mahogany table like a tumbleweed, and then collapsed in a tired little heap of grey dust.

"It wasn't in Montreal," she went on. "It was in Reno. He was getting a divorce. I was doing an act in one of the clubs. Like you said, he sat at a ringside table and fell in love with me. We had a nice six weeks. We had a little cabin on the outskirts of town and we had a lot of fun and never fought once till the night he left. Then I wanted him to take me with him and he wouldn't. I never saw him again. Now he's dead."

"You didn't look him up when you came to Montreal?"

She shrugged. "Ten years, after all. And he was married. I wouldn't know if he even remembered my name. I'm glad you told me he tore out my picture and saved it. I'm touched."

"Who was the girl he was divorcing in Reno?"

"I should know that? We had other things to talk about?"

"Where was he from, then?"

"Toronto, he said. But he wasn't going back there. I think he came to Montreal after he left me. I think that's where he said he was going." She got up. "What do you drink?"

I started to say rye. Then I decided I didn't feel quite at home, so I told her beer, the way one does in a cheap bar. Let's see anybody do anything to a beer.

She went to the kitchen and things rattled. She came back with a glass of beer, and a glass with ice cubes and a Coke.

"Isn't it funny, how people show up out of Sark's past and then he gets it."

"What two people?"

"You. And Albert Geysek."

She laughed, with her mouth, but not with the baby blue eyes. "Geysek! He never shot anybody in his life."

"Where did you know Geysek?" I asked her very fast.

"In Reno," she said easily.

"He wouldn't shoot Sark? Maybe not, the police kind of think he did. But then, they haven't heard about you yet."

You can't make love on sectional furniture, but she was going to try. She got up easily, careful to let the negligee drift slowly open. Wide open. She was wearing black panties that were mostly lace and her hips were broad and flat and her stomach was smooth and taut-muscled flat. There was a wide area of clear white skin and then the cantilevered bra, which on closer look might just be an unnecessary attempt to improve on nature. She came to me and knelt beside me and put her arms over my knees.

"The police don't have to know about me, do they?" she asked softly, and the eyes pleaded. "I don't know a thing about Sark's death. Really I don't. It's been ten years since I had anything to do with him. But the cops would come here and stick their noses into all kinds of things that had nothing to do with the killings. And it might make an awful lot of trouble for me."

"The cops might want to know about this set-up, eh?"

She hung her head bashfully, so I'd see the way her long eyelashes swept her cheek.

"Who's daddy?"

"No one. I mean, no one who means anything to me. An old friend."

"Sure. All you girls have old friends. Do I look as if I were still in college?"

Her hands came up my sides and exerted a gentle pressure, bending me toward her. "I only want to be left alone." She strained toward me. There was no foam rubber in the bra. Her full lips were parted, glistening, trembling with desire.

Desire for what? Desire to keep away from the cops.

"All right, so you're a nice lay," I said. "My weakness happens to be beer. And when you met Geysek in Reno, he was plunk in the middle of a twenty-year stretch in an upstate New York pen."

She stood up. I stood up too. Something in the baby blue eyes told me I better be in position to dodge. But the beer made me a little slow and before I could move she slashed her hand across my eyes. I felt the scraping pain through the calm, quiet feeling I'd built up with all that beer. I saw green and purple blobs explode in front of my eyeballs. My beer was in my hand and it splashed and foamed in the glass like the Atlantic against rocks, while I swayed. Then I caught her hand before she could slap me again.

Faster than a revolving door pushed by a kid, she clutched my arm with her other hand and brought it to her mouth and bit the wrist with her white, even teeth. The beer went on the rug. Her teeth were sharp. They sawed raggedly through my skin.

That was enough. I twisted a hand in her smooth blonde hair and jerked her head up and back and away from me until her neck cracked. Her teeth came out of my wrist and there was an animal, grinning grimace on her face, like a dog when you haul it out of a fight by the scruff of its neck. Her pupils had dilated until the blue of her eyes was lost in black. I slapped her twice, back and forth across the face, and blood from my torn wrist splattered her cheeks. I hit her on the mouth, cutting her lips against the straight teeth. And the apartment door opened.

I turned in time to see the two torpedos coming for me. If they were part of her family, I'd take the Geek brothers for mine. One was small and wizened and middle-aged, and his face had been hit by everything from saps to spinnakers. He looked like somebody's chauffeur gone wrong. The other was built like a Christian slave who had just finished off three lions in the Arena. I untangled my hand from the blonde's hair and threw her away; she plastered herself against one of the olive-green walls and stayed plastered. I went to my knees under the grabbing claws, and got one arm to my head in time to protect it as the battered old chauffeur fell over it. The chauffeur sprawled on the floor and looking back kicked at my head with one foot. He landed two kicks before I could roll away from him.

The Neanderthal had stepped back after missing once. Out of his pocket came a horn case that he opened to show a blade big enough for skinning elk. He had fought with that knife often. He didn't make the mistake of raising his arm. He held the blade low, ready to gouge upward with it, and crouched toward me.

I rolled over on the chauffeur, and over again pulling him on top of me to get him between me and the knife. I kneed him in the belly to knock out his wind and he went limp with a gasp.

I got one knee pulled up under me for leverage and lifted him and bowled him at the gorilla's legs. The gorilla dodged, and I had time to scramble up and grab a table. The gorilla threw his knife. The blade buried an inch of its length in the mahogany.

I edged toward a window. The lower sash was open and the space was covered by a rusty screen. I caught a glimpse of a porch roof below. I threw the table at the gorilla and jumped sideways through the screen.

I hit the porch roof rolling, and I rolled to its edge and dropped onto grass. I lost my wind like a burst balloon. I lay still for a minute. Nothing hurt quite enough to be broken.

Before the gorilla could get downstairs and into the backyard, I was over the alley fence and gone. I went to a garage and gave my keys to a boy and told him to go pick up the Riley.

I hadn't eaten since Tuesday dinner and this was Wednesday at six. I suddenly felt as though eating was a good idea. I went down to a Honey Dew on St. Catherine Street and had breakfast, just to warm up. Then I went to Slitkins and Slotkins and had a good steak dinner.

Scene Eight

Herbinger's Pharmacy, 4055 Cote Ste. Catherine Road, was as modern as the Toronto subway.

I parked the Riley across the street and walked in. The place was inhabited by a soda jerk wearing a white jacket, and a deadpan fountain girl. I picked the soda jerk. "Where's Mr. Herbinger? In the back room?" I asked him.

"Yeah, I guess so."

"Which way?"

"You a detail man?"

"Sure. Ayerst. Which way?"

"Through the door beside the drug counter, over there."

Stepping from the store into the little dispensary was like going from a model modern house into the Victorian room of a museum. There was nothing in the place that had been new even fifty years ago. Beside the door was an old roll-top desk. Down the side wall were marble-topped lab benches and an old lead sink with a dark, tarnished old fashioned gooseneck faucet. He must have had the modern plumbing ripped out of here and put in the sink, brought like everything else from an old store he'd once had, for sentiment's sake.

The near side wall was shelved and the shelves were crammed with bottles of drugs. At the end of the room the old man himself sat on a high, rickety wooden stool, weighing out drugs on an antique balance with weights on one pan and a little metal weighing boat on the other. He was tapping a powdered drug from a scarred horn spoon into the boat.

I could just see his back. He was a chubby man with pure white hair, a little frayed around the edges, and the back of his neck and his ears that stuck out a bit were ruddy red. He was wearing a white coat and his legs were tucked up, with his feet on a rung of the stool, and he was whistling clearly and softly something that sounded like 'Ah So Pure' from Sampson and Delilah.

The doorway I'd come through was curtained, and I'd made no noise. He didn't seem to know I was there. He didn't turn around and he kept on with his work. He took a spoonful of a white crystalline powder from a big bottle beside his pan balance and tapped the side of the horn spoon so the powder fell into the weighing boat, until the scale balanced. Then he put the spoon into the bottle, picked up an open medicine capsule, shoved a tiny funnel into it, shook the powder from the boat into the capsule, and sealed it. He put the capsule in a small white box. When he had five capsules in a box he folded paper over them and closed the box. He tucked the box into an open briefcase that lay on the marble-topped bench to the right of the scale. Then he started all over again on another box.

It wasn't interesting after the first two boxes, but I was afraid to speak. He looked pretty old and a sudden fright wouldn't do him any good. He finished 'Ah So Pure' and started on the 'Prelude' to the Third Act of Lohengren, weighing away. After a few more minutes, without even looking up from his work, he said, "Good evening." So I'd been worried about startling him, so I almost jumped out of my own skin.

I approached his stool. "Good evening, Mr. Herbinger."

"What can I do for you, Sir?" He had a quiet, cultured voice.

"I'm a private investigator," I said. The truth was all right here, I thought. "My name is Teed. I wonder if I could ask you a few questions in connection with a case I'm working on."

"Why, certainly," he smiled. He put the fifth capsule into one of the little boxes and closed the box. He put it in the briefcase and locked the briefcase. He put a ground glass stopper in the bottle he had been weighing the powder from. Then he got down on his hands and knees and opened a small safe that was sitting on the floor beneath his bench. He put the bottle and the briefcase in the safe and slammed the door and twirled the knob. "Sorry," he said apologetically. "Always have to put that stuff away. Can't leave it lying around of course. Diamorphine hydrochloride."

"Oh. Poison?"

"Oh, yes."

"Why the briefcase?"

"I beg your pardon?"

"I'm sorry," I said. "Just an unnatural curiosity."

"Not at all," he said. "I supply the drug in specified doses to a private nursing home in the neighborhood. I'll be taking these capsules over there tomorrow."

"I see. About those questions."

"Certainly, Mr. Teed."

"I'm just chasing a wild lead, Mr. Herbinger. I'm trying to find out who owns a certain cottage in the Laurentians. The only thing I have to go on, besides a car license number I haven't looked up yet, is a bottle I saw in a room of this cottage. It was a bottle from your drug store."

"Which might have been bought by anyone, and carried up there, of course," he mused.

"Yes. Except that it was a prescription bottle."

"Ah. Did you take down the prescription number from the bottle?"

"There was no number."

"That's curious! Are you sure it was a prescription?"

"It said, 'One teaspoonful after meals, as required,' and it was in a four-ounce druggist's bottle."

"Just where did you find this bottle?"

I told him where the cottage was, and he laughed.

"Everything is explained," he chuckled. "That is a mild antacid I prescribed for myself. That is why it has no number. My dear boy, you've been in my cottage on Diamond Lake. How did you get up there?"

"A very long story," I said. "May I sit?"

"Forgive me. Of course." He got off the stool and we went across the room. He bobbed a bit as he walked, the way stubby stout met do. He sat down at the roll-top desk and I sat beside it.

"You have heard of John Sark?"

"I have heard his name a few times before today. After this morning, of course, I expect almost everyone in the city knows about him."

"Just before he was shot, he'd been carrying in his pocket a rough map showing the way to your cottage."

"Merciful heaven!" Herbinger gasped.

"I followed the map to your cottage. I found the bottle, and that brought me here. Could you tell me how Sark would know about your Laurentian spot?"

Herbinger stood up abruptly. "Of course not," he said. "I thought this was to be a long story, Teed. I think there is no more than this to it. Sark somehow stumbled on

my cottage, perhaps while he was driving in the Laurentians, and was struck by its quietness or its seclusion. The
map was drawn by hand? He may have made it himself,
so he could return. Or a friend of his did just what I
speculate John Sark did, and gave the map to him.

"You followed the map. I presume you were looking
for a clue to Sark's murder. You found an old bottle which
led you here, to the owner of the cottage. But that is all,
Mr. Teed. I assure you there is no connection between
myself and John Sark except coincidence."

He could stand up if he wanted to, but I wasn't
standing. I wasn't through. "There's too much coincidence
in this affair," I said half to myself. Then I told him, "But
it is a long story, Herbinger. It isn't finished. You have a
daughter? A very beautiful brunette girl?"

"No." Very short with that, he was.

I pulled out my notebook and thumbed it. "You have
a car with the license number 53-633?"

"No!" he said. Then he suddenly got very tired and
sat down again in his chair. "Yes," he said. "I presume you
can trace that easily. The girl is not my daughter. She is
my niece. Her name is Pamela Hargrove."

"I see," I said wisely. I printed 'Pamela Hargrove' in
my book, for something to do. Below that I printed 'Carol
Weller.' It was beginning to work out a little bit. Like a
bridge hand after the dummy goes down, but before the
play begins.

"She is my sister's only child. My sister and her husband have been dead for a number of years and she has
made her home with me. I am a bachelor. I am also being
a talkative fool, Teed. What do you want to ask?"

"I think you know. Pamela was at your cottage about
five o'clock this morning. Why did she go there at that
hour?"

"To fish," Herbinger said, and he didn't seem to be kidding.

"At that time of the morning?"

"Certainly. She loves fishing. She very often goes up there alone to be out on the lake at dawn. That is when the fish bite best. I'm afraid you are not a fisherman."

"God forbid," I said. Reverently. "All right, she went up there to fish. I reached the lake just at dawn. She'd decided not to fish. She had been to the cottage and returned to the shore. She was leaving. She did her best to get me to leave too. But I stayed around. I went over to the island, and in the cottage I found a dead man, Herbinger. A man who had been murdered. You'll read all about it in tomorrow's morning paper, so I won't spoil the story for you. But that's what I found on the island. Besides the bottle."

"I – knew," he admitted. He had gone dead white. "She told me about it. But she didn't kill the man, Teed. You must believe that. You must."

"I'm being asked to believe a lot," I remarked. "That you and the Sark never knew each other, though he carried a map to your cottage in his pocket. That your niece just happened to go up there to fish on the morning a man was killed there. Next you'll want me to believe you don't know who was shot in your cottage."

"God's truth, I don't Teed," he said tensely.

"All right," I said, sounding as tired of it as I was. "I'm not going to get tough with you, Herbinger. I'm not going to threaten you. I haven't told the police your niece was at the lake when I found the body, because I want to hear her story first. I'm as interested in solving this killing as the police are, and if I'm not as thorough, I'm sometimes faster. If Pam is frank with me, I'll try to keep her out of it for the present if she doesn't belong in, that is. You'll get a call from the cops when they find out the cottage belongs to you. That's all."

I got up. "The body on your island was the Sark," I told him.

"What do you mean? The Sark was killed in his apartment."

"Maybe he was. Maybe his double was. He had a double. Or did you know? Nobody knew, according to them. I'm getting damned tired of stupid bastards that don't know anything. Pardon me. I'm tired and puzzled and I feel older than you do. Sark or Sark's double was murdered on your island. And somebody will hang for it sooner or later. With these kind words, good night."

Scene Nine

THERE WAS A BACK WAY to the Scaley house. Coming along Cote des Neiges from the north you turned up the side of Westmount, instead of going onto Westmount Boulevard and tackling it from the front. The road you took climbed, banked, curved, hair-pinned, hung over the edge of a reservoir and eventually came out on Belmont Terrace. It was dark enough now to make me want to stop there and look down on the city. The city was beautiful by night, or by day, from the heights. That was why I lived as high up as I could, and had a terrace off my apartment.

I sat in Riley and looked at the winking lights. Somewhere down among them was the character who had killed both the Sarks. Or somewhere right here. We were beginning to have a promising list of suspects. Albert Geysek. Martha Scaley. The little man in the white coat who answered Scaley's bell. Inez Scaley. Carol Weller. The two torpedos who jumped me. The Sark's bodyguards; maybe they were the torpedos. I sort of thought they were. Also, Pamela Hargrove. And Herbinger. That made nine.

Probably MacArnold did it.

He wasn't the most logical suspect, though. Who was the most logical suspect? Who was right there on the scene of the crime both times? Sure.

R. Teed.

R. Teed had a lot of work to do before the cops realized that.

I got out of Riley and buzzed the Scaley bell. The

current tickled the spine of the little man in the white coat and he came just as I took my finger off the button.

"Mrs. Scaley," I told him.

"I'm sorry, Mr. Teed, she's not at home this evening," he said. He was polite but he wasn't afraid of me.

"Did she leave a note or any kind of message for me?"

"No, sir."

"You'll do," I said, "I'd like to ask you a few questions."

"Certainly, sir." He stood aside and let me come into the great dim dark-panelled hall.

"What is your name?" I asked him.

"Martin, sir."

"What's your last name, Martin?"

"Froste, sir. Froste, with one 's' and an 'e.'"

"What time did Mrs. Sark get home last night?"

"It was very late, sir. I sat up for her, but I'd been dozing. I'm afraid I didn't glance at the clock as she came to the door. After I opened the door for her I went back to my own rooms and went to bed. It was just about two o'clock when I got into bed."

"I see. Who brought Mrs. Sark home?"

"I don't know, sir. When I got to the door she was alone. The car that had brought her was gone. She told me she had come home by taxi, after leaving her party at the Trafalgar because of a headache, but she said it was almost gone, and she was just going to go right to bed."

I knew damned well he had seen the Riley in front of the house last night, and I thought he was telling a very nice story. "Is this exactly what you told the police?" I wanted to know.

"Yes, sir."

"Did Mrs. Sark leave the house after you let her in?"

"Why, no, sir. Certainly not." This surprised him. "Not

until the police came and took her down to the ... the morgue."

"How do you know? You went to sleep, didn't you?"

"Yes, sir. But as you know, this is no longer Mrs. Sark's home. She is a guest here. She has no key to the front door. That is why I stayed up to let her in. If she had gone out again she would have had to ring me to get in."

"She could go out and leave the door unlatched, couldn't she?"

"No, sir," he said positively. "Mrs. Scaley is very particular about the way things are locked, since she lives here with just the servants. She had a special lock installed on the front door. It is permanently locked. There is no latch that can be left off. There is no way of opening it from the outside except with the key."

"Back door? Side door?"

"They are both locked with keys which I keep on a ring. I lock them at nine o'clock in the evening and unlock them again in the morning. One can go out only by the front door after nine o'clock unless I unlock one of the other doors."

"How about the garage? Mrs. Sark's car is here in the garage, isn't it?"

"Yes," he admitted. "That is the weak point in the house. The door from the house to the garage is not locked. If someone were to go out of the house to the garage, open the garage doors and drive a car away without closing them, the house would be open until they returned. Theoretically."

"Why theoretically?"

"My rooms are over the garage, sir, and I'm a very light sleeper. I have never failed to hear a car being taken out of the garage. One evening last week Mrs. Sark took her car out about ten o'clock. I came down to the garage immediately but she had remembered to close the doors after leaving. The lock was sprung. When she came back she rang for me. She knows, of course, that Mrs. Scaley hates to have any of the doors left unlocked."

"I see," I said. "So you could swear that Mrs. Sark didn't leave the house last night alone, after she came in."

"Yes, sir."

"Tell me something about yourself, Martin," I said.

"Certainly, sir. Anything."

"Well, go ahead then."

"I am a native of Montreal, though my parents came from England. A good many years ago, when Mr. Scaley established his metals firm in Montreal, I went to work there as an office boy. As the firm grew and I became older I was employed exclusively in assisting Mr. Scaley. I was the general handyman in his private office, I drove his car and attended to small details for him. When he retired he asked me to come here. I had no family and was most willing to comply with his wishes. I have been in this house for nearly a decade."

"That's complete enough. You say you had no family. I assume your parents were dead by this time —" he nodded — "and you hadn't married."

"I had married, sir, but I had lost my wife."

"No children?"

"No, sir."

"And when did you first meet John Sark?"

"I didn't exactly meet him, of course, sir. I first saw him when he came here to the house to call for Mrs. Sark and when he came here as her guest."

"And you hadn't heard about him before that?"

"No, sir," he said. He flushed.

He was lying. And I didn't know why.

I felt sorry for him. He was an innocent, respectful, respectable little man who had been faithful and helpful to one Scaley after another all his life, never doing much living of his own, never taking too much on his own shoulders like some servants try to, never letting his people down. And he was lying to keep me from getting a lead on who killed the filthy Sark, because perhaps Sark was plugged by someone he liked, who had a good reason for killing the lump.

I felt sorry for him. But he was the third little bastard who had amused himself lying to me that day and I felt a little bit sorry for myself too.

"I won't waste any more time on you," I said. "When you feel you can tell me the truth, call me up."

"Yes, sir," he said in a dead voice. He was still red.

"Is Mrs. Sark at home?"

"Yes, she is in her room, sir. Shall I ask if she can see you now?"

"If you please."

He went out and upstairs. I didn't hear him come down again, but a few minutes later Inez came in. She looked like the wrath of Beelzebub.

She had been drinking alone in her room until her hands shook, and it hadn't made her drunk, just sickly.

"What happened?" I asked her.

"Nothing much, Russ. They came here about five this morning and Martin pounded on the door to wake me up. I wasn't asleep. There was a big man named Framboise. He was fairly decent. But they took me down to that God-awful morgue and made me identify John."

I didn't tell her she might have been looking at some unknown bum who happened to be Sark's double. Some people would think I was cruel, but I wasn't going to tell her about the double at all. I had to have a positive identification of Sark somehow, and maybe I'd get it when they showed Inez the second body – if it came as a surprise.

"It isn't as bad as you make it," I said, "he was cheating on you anyway."

She smoked most of a cigarette silently. She said, "You mean he was away with a woman those last five days? That doesn't matter too much. I'd already thought of that and got mad about it. I'd written that off."

"No, that's not what I meant. I meant you were never really married to him." I told her the story I'd got from Carol about Sark being in Reno for a divorce ten years ago, though I didn't say where I got it. "A Reno divorce is no good in Quebec," I told her.

"I expect he thought it was. Or he wouldn't have bothered to get one."

I said, "What happened after you identified the body?"

"They just asked me where I had been that evening. Just 'a routine check.' That was the way Framboise put it. I told them about the party I was with, and how I got a headache in the Trafalgar and took a taxi home. Then they brought me back here and quizzed Martin for a while."

"How did the story stand up?"

"Not worth a damn. Don't worry, you're not involved. They didn't have to talk to Bob. They hunted up the people I'd been with, and talked to them sometime today. Then they came back and grilled me again. The others remembered me leaving the Trafalgar about twelve-thirty, after the last round of drinks had been served and the bar closed for a while. And Martin told them I didn't get home until nearly two. The man who talked to me today wasn't

Framboise; I think his name was LaBelle. He was very nice too. He just wanted to know why it took me so long to get here in a taxi, when usually it only takes fifteen minutes."

"What did you say?"

"I had to change my story. I said the headache was very bad and I'd stayed in the ladies' room in the Traf for a long time, afraid I was going to be sick. I said I couldn't tell how long it was, but it might have been an hour. There's no attendant in the room, so they can't check that one way or the other. Then I said I went out and walked a block or two in the open air and felt better. After that I took a taxi home."

"When they checked up on your alibi did they establish that you'd been with your party continuously up until the time you reached the Traf?" I asked.

"I don't know," she admitted, "why?"

"I haven't too good an idea of the time of death, but I expect it was around midnight, just before you got to the Trafalgar. They'll probably have it set pretty closely. I hoped you were alibied at least up until the time I saw you."

"Sure," she said. "Not only for the sake of the police. But also so you won't have to suspect me."

"That's right."

"Well, I'm not. Make what you want to of it. I was separated from the party between eleven thirty and eleven forty-five. We left the Archers', where we'd been drinking, at eleven thirty and I didn't drive straight to the Traf with them. I said I wanted to go home for a minute to get a wrap, because I felt chilly. I wouldn't let anyone drive me. I picked up a taxi on the Boulevard."

"And came here?"

"No. And didn't come here. I was thinking of going to the apartment to see if John had come back. Just thinking of it. I had the taxi driver park in front of the Castle and I sat there trying to persuade myself not to go in. I did persuade myself. So I made him drive me to the Traf, and they were all waiting for me in the lobby and we went into the bar together."

"Oh, fine," I said. "Perfect. I suppose you couldn't have called the cab from the Archers', so there'd be some record of it. No. You wouldn't do that. You had to go out and catch it on the street. And there are only two thousand Diamond cabs in Montreal, so I suppose it was a Diamond."

"Yes, I think it was."

"Never mind. You didn't know Sark was going to get shot. Or did you?"

"That's not funny, Russell," she said angrily. It was the first sign of real life she'd shown.

"It's all right, anyway. Nobody in the party remembered to mention this to the police or they would have asked you about it. Or else they're sure he wasn't killed before midnight and aren't checking up on the earlier time."

"Or maybe they're just saving that bit to hang me," she said cynically.

"It isn't that bad. After I brought you home last night, what did you do?"

"I went upstairs and tried to sleep."

"You stayed in this house until the police came."

"That's right."

"According to Martin, you couldn't go out again without his knowing, anyhow. He'd have had to let you back in, because at night all the doors are permanently locked from the inside. Right?"

"Yes." she almost smiled. "Just because he's too old to climb through windows, he forgets other people can. The back windows are only two or three feet above the sidewalk. Or I could have gone out in my car. He sleeps in the rooms over the garage, but he sleeps like an opium-eater."

I got up to go. "Thanks for telling me," I said.

"I don't see what that has to do with anything."

"It has nothing to do with anything. Good night. Stay at home and be good. Call me if anything happens."

Martin was slipping. When I got to the front door he wasn't there to let me out. I whistled and he came out of the floor like a genie. "Give a message to Mrs. Scaley," I briefed him. "Tell her that her thousand is gone and then some. And what do I do now anyway?"

"Yes, sir," he said meekly. "I'll tell her, sir. Good evening."

Scene Ten

I GOT BACK TO MY APARTMENT. It was half-past ten. I went to the frig for a beer and there wasn't any beer. Then I remembered I'd skipped lunch in the ten minutes between breakfast and dinner, and I am not a man to let uneaten meals sneak away unnoticed. I snipped up a few rashers of bacon fine with scissors and dumped them into the griddle. When they were hissing hot but not crisp I threw two eggs on top of them and scrambled everything together and seasoned it with salt and fresh-ground pepper and tarragon, the herb that smells like the essence of new-mown hay and makes eggs taste like morning in the country. The dish was faster than an omelet and heartier. I ate it with a glass of milk and Scotch, just enough Scotch to give the milk a proper tang.

I thought. I thought about the three people who had lied to me in one way or another and the one person who'd told the truth, whole and nothing but. The three liars, Carol, Herbinger, and Martin, couldn't all have killed the Sark. So maybe Inez had.

And maybe she hadn't. There was somebody else connected with the case, maybe distantly but connected, who hadn't been turned up yet. Not Albert Geysek; someone new. I had thought about him. Then I mixed another Scotch and milk, this time just enough milk to dilute the Scotch, which was Berry's Best and didn't need much diluting. I went to the hall and unplugged the phone. I brought it in and plugged it in again in the front room beside the chesterfield and lay down and thought some more. Then I phoned Danny Moore, who took medicine at McGill when I was there.

"Hi, Dan, it's Russ," I said. "How's Glady?"

"Eight-ninths happy," he said. "Where've you been Russ? Why not come around and call on a couple in confinement?"

"Say, I'd like to. But I'm working through sleep and waking on a case."

"Best excuse I've heard tonight. How are you?"

"Fine," I said, "and what is diamorphine hydro-chloride?"

"Diamorphine hydrochloride is heroin. Do you know what heroin is?"

"Yes, thank you, I know what heroin is." I insulted him a few times to get even and hung up.

Heroin. I thought so.

Before I went any further with that one, I called Telephone Answering Service just to check in. There hadn't been any calls at my office through the day. And I called Framboise, also just to check up. "Why haven't you taken Inez down to look at the body from the island?" I asked him. "I went to see her. I might have let something slip."

"You are sure you did not?" he asked anxiously.

"I didn't say a word about the second body."

"They were working on 'im today. Finding bullets. Also, the case is my *enfant* and I asked to be 'ere when she saw 'im. I am going to get 'er now."

"Go easy with her. She's in worse condition than the wreck of the *Julie Plante*."

"Sure," he said. Then, grudgingly, "I 'ave to make to you an apology besides. You were right. Undoubtedly the men were doubles. It is, you would say, huncanny."

I agreed with him. I accepted his apology. He had nothing new except the bullets which had gone through the body in the kitchen, which were .45s, and the bullet from the head of the corpse in the cottage, which was also a .45 slug.

He was looking for Sark's two bodyguards, but they hadn't been picked up yet. He wasn't looking for Carol Weller because he didn't know about her yet. He didn't know about Pamela Hargrove either. They had checked on ownership of the cottage and someone would be calling on Herbinger in the morning.

I felt a little guilty not telling him about Carol and about Pam, but it was something like struggling with an algebra problem. When you got halfway through and it looked like there was a solution somewhere, you got stubborn as hell about solving it yourself. You wouldn't take it to the professor for any money. I just wanted one more day.

One more night and day, that was, because I was still working. When I got through with Framboise I phoned the *Clarion* and got MacArnold. "Happy homicides," I said. "Did you talk Framboise into giving you an exclusive on that second corpse?"

"You didn't see anything in this afternoon's *Star*, did you?"

"Good enough. Say, I want a name I've forgotten. Friend of yours, I think a photographer. Runs a poker game in his apartment almost every night. You took me there once or twice."

"Crawford Foster," he said promptly. "Only it hasn't been poker lately, it's been craps. Want to go lose some money?"

"I could."

He gave me an address on Jeanne Mance and hung up after I declined to tell him anything I'd been doing since morning. I had a bit of luck there, because he hadn't been talking to Cassie.

I finished the Scotch and went down to the Riley. I drove along Cedar and Pine to Jeanne Mance and down it until I found the address, between Sherbrooke and Ontario.

On the way I was remembering what I knew about Crawford Foster. He was known as Crawfie. He was a freelance photographer, which meant he took pictures on assignment from companies and shops, was sometimes called in by a newspaper to cover a story when all their full-time men were busy, and went independently to such festivities as weddings and wakes, taking pics the papers might buy from him. He had an office and darkroom on St. François-Xavier Street, in a building that had been built about the year Montcalm lost Quebec, and he had this apartment.

The apartment was in the first floor of an old grey-stone house. A very old house. The walls luckily all leaned the same way, but they were visibly out of plumb. The floors were sagging and tremulous and there was a pervading stink of dead termites and rot. The termites had probably been poisoned by the rotten wood.

Crawfie got up from the crap game when I came in. he was five foot, four and one-half inches tall. He insisted on the half-inch. He was a little less myopic than a mole and about as chubby as a koala. He had thick yellow hair, small close-set eyes behind a pair of Winston Churchill horn-rims, and a mouth as big and full of teeth as the business end of a sileage chopper.

The room was big and high-ceilinged. It had no floor covering, curtains, pictures on the walls, nor any furniture to speak of. Plaster had fallen from a few places on the ceiling and out of the network of jagged cracks on the walls, leaving the naked lathes to grin uncomfortably into the room. Perhaps some of the plaster that had fallen in the last ten years had been swept up, but the floor hadn't been scrubbed in that time. Crawfie couldn't be poor enough to live in the place. Maybe he thought it was Bohemian.

About eight men, all of them more or less connected with press work, squatted or knelt on the filthy floor in a circle playing craps; a cloud of smoke hung low over the group. I could see most of the faces dimly. I knew two or three of them and I'd seen the others around town.

There were quarts and glasses of beer on the floor beside the players. Every little while a beer glass would get knocked over and the whole circle would shift a foot or so away from the slop until it dried into the floor. I took a quart of Dow from Crawfie, refused a glass, and cut into the circle beside the place he resumed.

The boys were playing with bills, not silver, but it wasn't a big game. Ones, twos, an occasional five-bet. Crawfie got the dice and made two passes on a nine and a six. He drew some money, crapped, and passed the dice.

I put out a dollar and gave the dice a long, honest roll. They gave me back a pair of ones.

Crawfie had covered me. "Snake-eyes," he said gleefully, and picked up the money.

I looked at the dice resentfully I put out a two and Crawfie covered again. I blew on the dice and muttered to them, "Come on, leetle marbles. After a crap a natural. Show me a six and a five, count up to *e-leven*."

The dice rolled six and six. I was colder than liquid hydrogen. Crawfie crowed and picked up his money, and I grimaced and passed the dice. They went on around the circle.

I drank beer from the bottle and made a little money on side bets. The dice came back to me in about fifteen minutes. I started with two this time, and got nine for a point. It came right back on the second roll. I left the four dollars. Then I sevened.

Someone yelled from the other side of the circle, "The guy's gettin' hot. With him for two."

"Cover the center first," Crawfie said loudly. There were eight simoleons of mine to be covered, and covered they were. I rolled a six and nearly wore the spots off the dice making the point. That should have been a warning, but I drew just two dollars and left fourteen in the center. Twenty-eight piastres, or nothing. I was beginning to get a little excited. It wasn't the money as much as the game. I shook the dice a long time and talked to them and rolled.

Snake eyes again.

My excitement degenerated to a slight headache. I passed the dice I got up and wandered to the can.

Crawfie didn't keep coal in his bathtub. That was the only good thing you could say about his lavatory. The bowl of the toilet was cracked. Most of the enamel was chipped off the wash basin and what was left was stained a dirty brown. The mirrored door of the medicine cabinet had been ripped from its hinges in a past epoch and was on top of the toilet tank, leaning against the filthy wall. Inside the exposed medicine cabinet were a shaving brush with dried soap caked on it, a tube of shaving cream and a tarnished razor, two dog-eared toothbrushes and a tooth paste tube, uncapped, with its tongue hanging out; a bottle of Aspirin tablets, a dirty glass, a bottle of Vatronol nose-drops, and a small white box. The box was about an inch square and a half-inch high. It was unlabelled. It had been sitting there waiting for me. I took it out of the cabinet and opened it. There were five capsules inside. Each of the capsules was filled with powder. White, crystalline powder.

I put the box back. I went out and rejoined the party.

Somebody coming in to join the game had brought a midnight edition of the *Clarion* and I picked it up. MacArnold's story had rated a two-column head and a byline, on the front page. Crawfie came up behind me and looked over my shoulder while I ran through the first paragraph.

"So they found a double to the Sark!" he exclaimed.

"Yeah, unless the second one was the Sark himself."

I gave him the paper and he read intently for a minute, squinting his weak eyes behind the big glasses. "I bet the second body was the Sark," he said. "Somebody threatened him, perhaps Geysek as MacArnold suggests. So he pulls out and leaves the double to take the rap. Geysek, or whoever it was, shoots the double and then finds he's made a mistake. Maybe he even drags that out of the double before he shoots him. So he follows Sark and plugs him too."

"How does he know where the Sark has gone?"

"How did the police know? They found him."

"No," I said. "I found him." I explained about the map.

"Just where was this place?" Crawfie asked. His face had darkened with worry.

"Out of Morin Heights, on an island a few miles off the Sixteen Island Lake road. An island in Diamond Lake." Crawfie's mouth dropped open. His big, ugly teeth hung there exposed to the air like two rows of cod fillets drying on flakes. "My God," he gulped, "that's Uncle Eddie's cottage!"

"Sure," I said. "Uncle Eddie. That would be Uncle Eddie Herbinger."

He hadn't thought of my tying it up that fast. He looked at me and his face was ridiculous, like the face of a man caught on the street with his pants unzippered. "Ah ... ah ... ah ... " he stuttered. "Not really my uncle. Old friend of the family. How do you know whose place it was? That isn't in the story."

"The things they let MacArnold print are the things they doen't want to find out more about."

"So he was killed at Eddie Herbinger's. That doesn't connect Eddie with it."

"No," I said. "Maybe not. Nobody said Eddie was connected. Not directly anyhow."

"Not any way at all. Eddie Herbinger wouldn't have anything to do with that type of guy."

"He knows you."

Crawfie put the horse's teeth and the big wide grinning mouth to use. "What a humorist! And I thought you came here because you liked me, not for the money you make at craps."

"Speaking of crap," I said, "cut it out. Come into the can."

He followed me. Everything was in the same place in the bathroom. Shave kit. Toothbrushes. Toothpaste. Aspirin. Glass. Nose-drops. But no little white box.

Everybody was drinking beer. Everybody had been in and out of the place regularly through the evening.

"Okay, which one is the hophead?" I asked him. "Pretty hard for me to tell. I don't know enough about the stuff. Or maybe he was just getting it for a customer. Maybe there was enough in the box for a retailer to sell to all his customers."

Crawfie looked at me bug-eyed. He stopped trying to smile.

I said, "Eddie shouldn't have told me so much. It was a nice story, but he didn't have to tell me. Or tell me what the stuff was."

Crawfie lit himself a cigarette and looked at it. His fingers weren't trembling any more than a light floor under a rotary press.

"So I came here tonight to play craps. So I've been here before for that. Funny, the little things a person will notice. Like small white boxes in a medicine cabinet, when you're washing you hands. I wondered what was in those boxes, Crawfie. Nice to leave things lying innocently about, but don't underestimate the curiosity of your visitors. Don't underestimate coincidence, either."

I took the cigarette away from Crawfie's damp hand and threw it in the toilet. "So I came here tonight to play craps," I said again. "Uncle Eddie, is it? How does it tie up?"

He got an ectoplasmic wraith of his smile back. "Why, there isn't anything to tie up. What kind of story was old Eddie telling?"

"All about diamorphine hydrochloride. Heroin. Dope."

"Tie up. What do you mean, tie up?"

"Not between you and Sark, unless he was in the sniff racket too. Right now I don't care who sells dope to whom. I just want one thing. I want who killed the two Sarks."

"How would I know?"

"I don't say you know. I say you might suggest."

"But ..."

"You could suggest why Sark decided Eddie's cottage would make a good hideout. Maybe you could think of someone who knew Sark well and Eddie well. Or some connection, even, that made Eddie friends with Sark. Or with Sark's wife or double or one of his bodyguards."

"But he wasn't. There's no connection."

"There's got to be a connection somewhere."

"Then I don't know it."

"You aren't trying hard enough," I said. I waited, but that didn't produce anything. "All right, good night," I said. "The boys in the red coats will call after I leave."

"God be my witness, I don't know any connection between Eddie and Sark, Teed! You saw my yap fall open when you told me he was killed at Eddie's. Why would he be there? How the hell could he even find his way there?"

"I told you. Somebody drew him a map."

"But who? I don't know. Sark wasn't anywhere near this racket Eddie and I were in. Look, I'll tell you all I know about it. I know the broad outline. No detail. The goof comes in on ships from Europe ..."

"I thought it usually came from the Orient."

"Maybe, but the stuff we get comes from Europe. The big business is smuggling it into the States. I don't know how that's done. I think the island in Diamond Lake figures in it."

"As a delivery point?"

"It could be that. That end is handled by someone else."

"How do you know it isn't the Sark — wasn't the Sark?"

"Because I know who it is. Name something like mortuary. I think ... Mortland. Yes, Mortland. That's the name."

"And where do you come into the racket?"

"Eddie is just a broker in the business. The stuff comes in, he sends it out — to the lake. I've delivered it to the lake sometimes. Mortland takes over there. But of course, there's some local business."

"Enough to make five new millionaires, I bet."

"Enough. So Eddie distributes the stuff, locally. Teed, you can't blame me too much. I found out about all this ..."

"When?"

"Just after Eddie opened his new store."

"*When*, goddamn it?"

"That would be about three years ago."

"How did you get to know him?"

"I met him in the old days, when I lived in Ontario."

"What's the rest of the story? Or maybe I can fill it in from what I know about small-time grifters. You suddenly found Eddie was willing to pay through the nose to keep you quiet. That meant there had to be big dough in the thing. So you wanted it. So, you slimy little bastard, how many of your friends have you caught? You, the genial host. Always a crap game. Always a free beer supply. Always a little sniff lying around for anyone with the inclination and the dough. How many, Crawfie? Why didn't you ever ask me to try some?"

"Teed, I swear ..."

"Quit it," I said. "As of tonight. You're through."

His eyes narrowed and brightened. "You won't turn me in?"

"Sure I'll turn you in," I said. "I don't say when, that's all. What I have right now is two dead crooks and a drug ring. I want to clean up the two stiffs first. Then I'll look around.

"I had nothing to do with murder. Believe me."

"Sure, I believe you. I believe Stalin wants peace."

"I can't help you with these murders. I can help you with the drug racket. I can finger Herbinger and Mortland for you. You'd never get evidence on them without me."

"I don't have anything to do with cleaning up dopers," I said. "That would be the boys with the red coats and the bush hats. The mounted gentlemen."

"Well, when you tell them, tell them about me. Tell them I'll help them get evidence."

I was sorry there were witnesses so close. If we'd been alone I could have beaten him to a pulp. As it was I didn't want to touch him and do just half a job. I swallowed it.

"Where do I find Mortland?"

"He lives on the Sixteen Lake road, the first house on the left past the turnoff to Diamond Lake."

"Is he Eddie's boss, or vice versa?"

"He's Eddie's boss."

"Don't tell him you talked to me," I warned Crawfie. "I may want to kind of surprise him a little bit."

He tried to smile as he saw me out. He couldn't.

Scene Eleven

I SHUFFLED ALONG the corridor to my apartment door. I hadn't been so tired since we marched around Jericho six days running, blowing trumpets so the walls would fall down.

I keyed the lock and opened the door and dropped in. After a while I felt strong enough to crawl down the corridor to the living room. I even had enough strength to pull the switch and put the lights on.

It was the nicest living room I could put together and I liked it. One wall was dark brown and the others were a heavy cadmium yellow. There was a very dark green Indian rug on the floor. Along two of the yellow walls was a rambling low bookcase-cum-everything of dark brown painted wood that I had made to measure in the basement workshop.

There were the usual tables, in blond walnut; lamps with straight drum shades the color of the rug, and a chesterfield suite of yellow-green that a woman would call chartreuse. It was all the way I'd planned it and bought stuff and put it together, and I liked it all. All except the dirty feet of the man lying on the light green chesterfield.

It was the chauffeur-type torpedo. Not dead, asleep.

I needed something before I could cope. I went to the kitchen and opened the liquor cabinet and looked. I shook my head. I got the coffeepot out and boiled some coffee. When it was made I drank a cup black, and then brought two cups into the living room.

If he was laying for me he wouldn't come in and go to sleep on my chesterfield. I could go over him for hardware before I woke him up, but the risk seemed small enough to take. I sat where I was and whistled through my teeth at him.

He opened one eye and looked at me. He took his feet off the chesterfield and sat up and stretched. There wasn't any dirt where his feet had been. Lucky for him.

He looked at the coffee. "Thanks," he said. "I take cream and sugar."

"Then go the hell into the kitchen and get cream and sugar."

He went to the kitchen. After a while he came back without the coffee cup, but with a drink of whiskey. "I couldn't find any cream," he explained. He sat down on the chesterfield again.

A broken nose gives a face a lived-in look. This face looked as though the nose, cheekbones and jaw had all been broken, on several occasions. It looked like an old cuspidor after a hard night in the bar.

He cuddled his glass in both hands and drank from it wrinkling his nose, like a battered rabbit. "I'm Creep Jones," he informed. "I used to work for the Sark."

"How the hell did you get in here?"

"Back door. Any time I can't come through a back door I'll stop working and take up crime."

"Ha. It had a chain on it."

"There's a little trick with them. I'll show you some-time."

"Who was the big piece of mattress stuffing with you before?"

"At Carol's? That was Matt Croll. He was Sark's man too."

"What was the idea of trying to rough me?"

"You were roughing Carol."

"Since when did you and Matt take on the job of looking after Carol? She told me she had nothing to do with the Sark for the last ten years."

Creep looked puzzled. "I don't know about that. I didn't know she was acquainted with the Sark at all. She's Matt's baby. He was a little mad at you."

"I'm a little mad at him too. I bruise easy."

"What would you do if you came in and found some lug handling your babe?"

"I'd find out who hit whom first."

"I bet you would."

"How did you know who I was?"

"You left your card." He pulled it out of his pocket. "Remember?"

"So I did. Well, welcome. What did you want to discuss?"

"Who killed the Sark?"

"Wait while I get my friend Sergeant Framboise here."

"I don't mean I'll tell you who killed him. I don't know. The last time I saw him he was getting out of a rowboat."

"On the island?"

"Yeah."

"Where was Matt?"

"He was waiting on shore in the car while I rowed the Sark to the island."

"Then did you and Matt drive right back to Montreal?"

"Sure."

"And what did you do?"

"I went to Louie Two's. He's a friend of mine. He says

you're okay."

"He's a friend of mine, too. Where did Matt go?"

"To the Spadina. To case the place and lock it up."

"Who was the guy that got shot in the Sark's kitchen?"

"I think his name was Butch. I never saw him. I knew there was a double, but he was kept under cover. Now let me ask the questions, will ya?"

"Sure," I said. "Go ahead."

"Which corpse was the Sark?"

"*What?*"

"The one in the kitchen, or the one on the island?"

"You just told me you took the Sark to the island."

"I thought I did. But when I think back over it careful, I ain't quite sure. Not if the two looked as much alike as the papers say. And if it wasn't the Sark I drove, it makes a difference. Because it was supposed to be the Sark. It means I'd have to ask Matt some funny questions."

"Why?"

"Because I drove and Matt sat in the back seat and talked to him. It was a dark night and if it wasn't Sark I wouldn't of known. He didn't talk much. But he talked enough so Matt would of known. So if he known and didn't say, something smells. That's why I want to find out."

"My God, I don't know which was which," I said. "I can make a guess, but so can you. Even the cops don't know them apart."

"They got fingerprints and everything."

"The Sark was never convicted of anything, you know that. So he was never printed. Look, start at the beginning and tell me all about it."

"There isn't much. I was down drinking in Louie Two's and I got a call from Matt. This was sometime after one in the a.m. Matt said the Sark wanted to go for a ride and I was to come quick with the car —"

"When had you seen Sark last before that?"

"Oh—sometime last week. What difference 'at make?"

"I heard he was hiding out for five days, before he got shot."

"I wouldn't know."

"I bet you wouldn't."

"Well, he was away from his apartment since last week. I dunno why. He was holed up in one of his clubs out of the city. He done that often before."

"Not since he was married, he didn't."

"Well, I don't know why. Look, you want the story?"

"Yes. Go on."

"I got that far and went up Cote des Neiges to the Castle and they come out. They told me where to go —"

"Which one told you?"

"Both of 'em. Sark pointed out the white rock and said that was where I should turn. After we got there it was like I told you."

He stood up. "An' all I want to know is, which was which?" he asked plaintively. "Which was which?"

"Aw, go ask the cops," I said. "Or go down to the morgue and look at them both and see if you can tell them apart. I couldn't."

"Maybe I could," he said mournfully. "But I don't want to go down there. Somebody would ask me who I was."

"Why not go tell the cops your story? They don't have a thing on you, they just want to hear what you have to say. They're looking for you, but they don't want to hang a rap on you."

"Matt wants we should keep away from the cops."

"That sounds fishy to me."

"It wouldn't, if you knew Matt. Keepin' away from cops is a habit with him. He says they always either want money or to put him in jail."

"I wouldn't be surprised. I may want to see him, though. Will you tell me where I can get to him?"

"Nah."

"Louie Two told you I was okay, remember?"

The little mug thought that over. "Tell you," he said. "You call Louie Two if you want Matt. He'll tell me and I'll get you together with him."

"All right. And if I find out which body was Sark's, I'll tell you."

"It's a deal."

He left the way he came, by the back door. He said he'd lock it from the inside after him, and I bet he did. But I didn't check. I went to sleep. Right in the chair, without getting undressed or anything. I slept maybe fifteen minutes. It just wasn't my night for sleep. This case just wasn't one for sleeping nights.

The doorbell rang.

I let it ring. After a while it stopped. Then my conscience bothered me. I went and opened the door to see if whoever rang was still there.

It was the dryad, and she was.

The dryad wore more clothes than when she had climbed glistening out of the woodland lake, but her lower lip was still fully exposed and it was more tantalizing than ever. The long black hair had been combed crisply back behind her ears. Her dark skin glowed in contrast to the crisp light-yellow summer dress of some linenish material. The dress was just tight enough to make you realize what kind of scenery it camouflaged.

She was a tall girl, right up to my shoulder.

"Hello, Pamela," I said. "Thank you for coming."

She was scared. "I should thank you," she said. "I didn't see my name in the paper, and the police haven't been asking for me."

I didn't answer. I took her hand and led her into the living room, looking at her all the way. I sat her on the chesterfield and sat beside her, and I fed her a State Express and took one and lit them. I was still looking at her, and she was embarrassed. She flushed and played with a pair of yellow gloves she carried.

Then she looked straight back at me with the big eyes that were dark brown, almost black, and said, "You were the only person in the world who could tie me in with the murder on the island. That was why I tried to scare you away from the lake. I'm glad you didn't scare. I'm glad you found him and they got him out of there. I'm sorry I was so nasty. You would know why after you went to the island."

"Yes, I would know why."

"This is a peace mission. I came to say I was sorry."

"Was that all?"

"Uncle Eddie said you wanted my story. I came to tell you the story. And I came to thank you any way I could for not telling the police I was there."

"Drink?" I asked her.

"No, thanks. But you go ahead."

"No," I said. "I've got a headache now. Trying to figure out who shot the Sarks. If it wasn't you."

"It wasn't. You must believe that, or you would have told about seeing me there. Or would you? Would you sooner —"

"Sooner nothing, and don't get suspicious," I said.

"I'm not thinking of cooking up a deal with you. I never was. As soon as I think you're even maybe guilty, we go see Sergeant Framboise. And we go see him eventually anyhow. Don't get the wrong idea. You didn't come here to be seduced to keep me quiet. You came here to tell me the truth and go home. Or go to the Homicide Bureau with me. The way I look at you has nothing to do with this business. Besides, I'm too tired. Besides. Well, what happened?"

"Here's the whole business. It's good to tell someone beside Eddie. I woke early yesterday morning and it looked like a good day for fishing. I often go fishing that early, and besides I left a note for Eddie to read when he got up, if that proves anything. I took the car and got to the lake about four. The boat wasn't in the boathouse. I wondered what was going on. First I thought of turning around and going home. Then I decided to get undressed and swim to the island."

"You really got undressed," I said. "You didn't expect to meet anyone on the island, did you?"

She blushed again. "It was dark," she said. "If someone had taken the boat over to the island I thought I'd just sneak it away and row it back to shore."

"Did you see another car anywhere near the boathouse? Anywhere near where you parked yours?"

"It was dark," she said again. "No, I didn't. It was probably hidden."

"When I got there I didn't see your clothes. Where'd you leave them?"

"In my car. Oh, I suppose you looked for them before I came out of the lake. They were under the driving robe."

"Go on," I said.

"I got to the island. I didn't see the boat at first, so I

climbed out of the water. I was standing there, looking in the direction of the cottage and wondering what to do next, when I heard two shots. One right after the other. Then someone ran out of the cottage and down to the shore near me, and got into the boat. I ducked. The gunner got the boat pushed off and rowed away. Later I heard a car start up, on shore, and lights wave around among the trees as it turned, and then it went away. It was beginning to get light. I went up to the cottage and looked in the front room. The body didn't belong to anyone I knew. I got back in the water and swam the hell out of there. Then I met you."

"Why weren't you a good girl? Why didn't you call the cops as soon as you got back to Montreal and tell them all about the body?"

"If I hadn't met you, I was going to do something just as good as that. I was going to get a party together in the afternoon and go up there for a swim. We'd find the body then and report it right away. But, because I saw you I was afraid to do anything. I sat and shivered all day today, expecting you'd gone to the island and found him and set the police on my trail. I expected to be picked up any minute, until you came to call on Uncle Eddie."

"Pardon me," I said politely, and went out to the kitchen. I hunted in the cupboard and found my biggest glass, the 18-ouncer. I put six ice cubes and four ounces of V.O. rye and two ounces of water in it and came back to the dryad. "You can change your mind if you want to," I told her. "I changed mine. I decided I needed this."

"No. Thanks all the same."

"All right. You've had your chance. You're going to need a drink in a few minutes, and you're going to have to go get it yourself."

"Please. You've been nice. But if —"

"Sure, I've been nice," I said bitterly. "I haven't turned you in. Since you came I've been acting as much like a gentleman as I know how. So what does it get me? Lies, and more lies. People have been running a contest all day to see who could hold out the most on me. Carol Weller. Uncle Eddie. Martin Froste. Crawfie Foster, the crummy little scum. I beg your pardon. He's probably a friend of yours. The scummy little crumb."

"I don't see what you —"

"Go on, damn it, talk. Tell me all about you."

She was puzzled, and she was nettled, but I stared her down. She got on with it. She talked.

"I was born in 1920. My parents died when I was five. Ever since then I've lived with Uncle Eddie. When I was small we had a housekeeper. Later on I kept house for him, and clerked in the store. We —"

"Where was all this?"

"In Hamilton," she said. "We came to Montreal three years ago. Eddie got this new store. It's doing very well. I still clerk in the store and I still keep house for him. The address is in the phone book."

"Boyfriends?"

"I'm not deformed."

"Any special one?"

"A special one until a few months ago. Then he was stolen. And I won't tell you his name. I haven't seen him lately."

"Thank you," I said. "That will do. Except for one thing. What is Mortland's first name?"

She broke down and cried.

She didn't throw herself face down on the chesterfield and sob. She didn't even make any noise. She just bowed her head and screwed up her beautiful face, squeezing her eyes closed. She put her hand over her eyes and the tears leaked through and shone on her smooth tanned cheeks. She shook a little bit.

When she straightened up and arranged herself again her face wasn't spoiled. She didn't wear any eye makeup and the tears dried without staining her brown face or reddening her eyes.

"He's Dwight Mortland," she said, "And I'm sorry. I'm sorry I cried, and I'm sorry I lied to you. I didn't think you knew this much. I was praying this wouldn't come out."

Her voice trembled. "Why did they have to shoot him on the island?" she asked wildly. "Why did they have to take him up there to shoot him?"

"I don't know," I said. "I don't even know who shot him. Maybe you do. But leave that for a minute. Just now I'm interested in you. You and your fishing trips. You went to the island to leave some dope there for Mortland, didn't you? And when you got there you found the boat was missing. So he was already on the island. Somebody had their signals crossed. Maybe one of you forgot about daylight saving time. So you swam over to find him."

She nodded.

"You must have known him pretty well."

"I could call to him from the water, couldn't I?" she asked, but she didn't really care what I thought. "I had to get to him. There had been a hitch. I was late."

"Sure. Anyway it was dark, like you said. Well, when you got to the island somebody else was there. With a gun. And then what went on?"

"The rest of the story is just as I told it. I don't know how you ever found out about the other."

"When everybody's lying there has to be a weak sister who can't stand up. This time it was Crawfie. I'm telling you so you can do whatever you want to with him."

"He's weak," she agreed.

"One thing. The gunner on the island. Was it a man or a woman? Think. Think of the footsteps crossing the veranda. Think of the way the oars were handled."

She thought. She shook her head. "I don't know."

"Thank you," I said. "Good night."

She got up, but she didn't go. She stood looking at me. "I can't leave it just like that."

"What other way is there to leave it?"

"You don't know about Eddie. None of this is his fault."

"No. He's just running dope. Good night."

"He couldn't help it. Look, ten years ago, in Hamilton, he tangled with a man. The man wanted him to handle dope and he wouldn't do it. They tried to persuade him every way they could. Some of the ways weren't pretty — they even tried to kidnap me. Finally they framed him. He was sent up for seven years of attempted murder."

"It's a nice frame, if you can do it."

"They did it. They waited until a prominent citizen ordered a prescription. They got to the delivery boy and switched boxes. The prominent citizen almost died of cyanide poisoning, and it was shown that he and Eddie had quarrelled, and the delivery boy never had the nerve to come clean. Eddie got the rap."

"I suppose this can be proved."

"The trial is on record, of course. That was what really happened. Eddie got out three years ago. He was bitter. And of course he couldn't get anything to do. He'd lost his license. Finally a drug ring approached him. A different ring, Mortland's crowd. He held out for a long time. I was working and we lived on what I made. Finally Eddie gave in. I couldn't stop him. They twisted somebody's arm and got him a license here in Quebec, and set him up in the store on Cote Ste. Catherine Road."

"The big man he crossed in Hamilton. Who would that be?"

"His name was Calloway. I don't know where he is now."

"How deep are you in this?"

"I ... don't know," she said. "I've taken parcels up to the lake sometimes. When I was going fishing. I really do fish up there. I didn't know what was in the parcels. But I know what I've been doing."

"Just incidentally, I didn't see any fishing tackle in the cottage. Nor in your car."

"It's there," she said wanly. "Would I try to lie now? It's in a little shed tacked onto the cottage beside the back door. Maybe you didn't look there."

"Did Eddie know Sark?"

"Eddie didn't know Sark. I didn't know Sark. Mortland didn't know Sark."

"How did he get the map leading him to the cottage?"

"I wish I knew."

"And you haven't any idea who killed him?"

"No, no, no," she said. "Except that Mortland is out. The last thing in the world he'd want would be to draw attention to the lake."

I got up. I felt sadder than the Tragedy mark. The most beautiful girl I ever met was probably no murderess, but she was a doper. She was mixed up with weak or misguided or bitter or even vicious fools who were playing around with the deadliest little capsules this side of pure radium.

She was weak or misguided or bitter or even vicious herself. It was an effort to remember that, but I had to remember it.

I shoved her down the corridor and out the door.

Scene Twelve

I GOT TO SLEEP at four, and I got woken up again at seven, and if I ever work on another homicide case I will work with the day man and not with the night man.

It was my own fault. Before I went to bed I unplugged the phone from the living room and plugged it in beside my bed. Better I had left it unplugged.

The phone rang. I sprang toward it and got it instantly. I got the thing off the cradle before the tenth ring even started. I mouthed, and it came out approximately, "Hrlmwo."

"*Allo, allo,*" said a bright voice. "*Framboise ici.* I 'ave something to interest you."

"No doubt," I said, "but none of the bombs hit this building. Call me back if a second wave comes over."

"You don't understand, we have 'im."

"Who? The third Sark? The blue one?"

"You don' make good sense this morning. We 'ave Geysek."

"It makes me very happy," I said happily. "Where'd you find him, if I'm not too invisible?"

"It is your language, but do you not mean inquisitive? He was in a cheap hotel down near Windsor Station. He was pick' up there yesterday morning, habout eleven."

"Why didn't you tell me yesterday?" I asked peevishly.

"I didn' know. He called himself Art'ur Gayran w'en we booked 'im. Yesterday morning the *femme de chambre* went in to make 'is bed in t'is hotel, but 'e was still asleep. T'ere was a gun on the floor beside 'is bed, so she got scare' and made the manager phone us. The boys brought 'im in for 'aving a gun without the permit. Las' night, just for routine like always, they fire a bullet from 'is gun, in the Ballistic lab, an' compare it wit' any we have aroun' not identified. So his is the gun that killed Sark. Both the Sarks."

I came awake with a snap. "They were both killed by the same gun?"

"Sure. T'at's important, eh?"

"Brother, it is to me."

"We are talking now to Geysek. Come down, hif you want to listen."

"Sure," I said. "Hold everything. Fifteen minutes. Oh, wait. Which corpse is which?"

"*Chalice*, we don' know yet. We bring Mrs. Inez Sark down to the morgue las' night an' we show her the body from the island. She says that is 'er husband. So I say, 'But of course, t'is is not the body you identify las' night. See the bullet 'ole in the head.' She doesn' say anything, so I show her the body from the kitchen again. She says then, 'But that is John!'"

"And you couldn't get any more from her?"

"Not'ing but *la hysterie*."

"That's what I thought. Hold it on Geysek. I'm coming."

Maybe twenty minutes later I shoved open the door of his office. It was a big office that he shared with three other men. There were two desks against the far wall and one against each side wall. All the desks were tidy except the one Framboise was sitting at, so the other Sergeants were day men. Two other Homicide boys were in the room, and Geysek. Geysek was talking.

Framboise motioned me into the room and I closed

the door and crawled up on the first desk I came to and leaned on my arm.

Geysek was saying, " ... but I still had some friends in Toronto, so that was the first place I went. They gave me some clothes and some money and the fare to Montreal. I got here on the Flier Tuesday night. Ten-thirty."

One of the Homicide men nodded. He said in French to Framboise, "That's right. We checked and found some people who remembered him."

He would be easy to remember. He was slight and medium height and white haired, and he looked like a man of distinction even without a glass in his hand. He had a wide, straight, high forehead and a large straight nose. He had white, even teeth.

"What did you do after the train got in?" Framboise asked.

"I went to my hotel and registered. I took my bag to the room and cleaned up. Then I had enough money to go out and get drunk, so I did. I started in the bar in the hotel. I met some other men there, but I didn't get their names. We went on to other bars. I've never been in Montreal before, so none of them were familiar. I got pretty corked. I suppose I got back to my room about four. That's why I was still asleep when the girl came in in the morning."

"Fine," I said to Framboise. "He's just what you wanted, isn't he? No alibi from eleven till morning. No alibi for either murder. And he had the gun. What about the gun?"

"So help me God," Geysek said, "I never saw that gun before."

Framboise said, "W'y did you come to Mo'real?"

"To get a job."

"You 'ad friends here?"

"I had John Sark. We used to be partners."

"There's a funny story went around about that," I said. "I don't like to speak evil of the dead, but the story is Sark crossed you when you were caught by the Yanks. He could have helped you, but he didn't. So you swore you'd get him when you got out."

"That's a fine story," Geysek said, shifting his gaze to me. "It would make a good movie. All that's wrong with it is first, the Sark did try to help me when I was arrested. Second, I wouldn't swear vengeance on anyone. I'm not that type. Ask the boys back in my college. Ask the boys I ate with and worked with and ask my cellmates. You know what I did in that pen? I ran the library. I had a gold star on my report card every month. Back when I took chances, I knew what I'd have to pay if I got caught. I don't blame Sark for anything. I was even hoping I might get a job from him. It's a little hard for an ex-con to get a job, except from an old friend."

"The Sark must have had a very bad conscience. Or maybe he was going soft in his old age. Because he was scared silly of you. He hired bodyguards a year before you got out of the stir. He even found himself a double."

"Yes," Framboise came in, "an' is it not funny, the night you come to town, the double of Sark is killed. Sark is also killed. T'en you are pick' up with the gun which does the killings."

"The gun that did both killings," I said. "Your boys are sure of that, are they, Framboise?"

"Ballistics report is lock' in the safe. Detailed. Photomicrographs of all the bullets. An' the expert will testify in court. Geysek, we will write up your story as a statement an' ask for you to sign it. Anyt'ing more?"

"No. It's all circumstantial evidence," And I haven't a damn' bit of proof to throw against it. Except proof that I never threatened to get Sark."

"It's nice circumstantial evidence," I said. "It would convince any jury."

"It's the nicest frame I ever heard of," Geysek told me. He didn't whine and he didn't look sorry for himself.

"Take 'im out," Framboise directed.

I said, "Hold it a minute." I looked straight at Geysek. "Do you want to retain me to investigate the murders of John Sark and an unidentified man, his double, of which you are accused?"

He looked straight back at me. "Yes," he said, "I want to retain you."

"Framboise, you heard that," I said. "Verbal contract, before witnesses. Perfectly legal. Can I talk to him alone?"

Framboise blinked. He was silent for a minute. "Sure," he said softly at last. "Sure, you dirty son of a bitch. You can talk to 'im alone. After we take 'im down an' put 'im in a cell you can go to the visitors room an' tell that you want to see Geysek. You represent 'im. I'm a witness to t'at. So you will see 'im."

He took the other two Homicide boys with him through the door.

"I don't know your name," Geysek said. Pleasantly.

"Russell Teed. Private investigations. You're something new to me. I never before had a client accused of murder."

"You stuck your neck way out. I don't know who hung this on me, but it was hung very prettily. I wouldn't even be surprised if the men I met in the bar were plants, left there to keep me out and unaccounted for the proper length of time."

"The police aren't going to try to find them," I said.

"I don't think I'll try either. I'd sooner prove who did it. I'll need help."

"Any little thing," he said.

"I'm going to repeat a list of names to you. Yell out if any of them mean anything."

"Go ahead."

"Sammy. No last name. He worked at Sark's Spadina club as a bookkeeper."

"That might be Sammy Menowitz," Geysek said. "Menowitz worked for Sark and me when we were partners in the twenties. He was a quiet little guy with a limp."

"That's the one. He was shot, too."

"When?"

"Sometime Tuesday night, before Sark and the double. By the way, did you leave any fingerprints on that gun? I don't mean did you use it. Did you pick it up?"

"I did not. The first thing I knew Wednesday morning there was a gendarme shaking my shoulder. There were two of them in the room and the other one already had the gun. He showed it to me and said, 'Is this yours?' I told him it wasn't, that I'd never seen it before."

"Okay. Second name on the list: Carol Weller." That didn't get me any reaction except a shake of his head, so I rhymed off some more. "Pamela Hargrove, Eddie Herbinger. Dwight Mortland. Matt Croll. Creep Jones. Stop me if I'm getting warm."

He shook his head again. "Maybe I've been out of circulation too long to be any good to you."

"Martin Froste. Martha Scaley. A man named Calloway. No?"

His head was still shaking. Slowly but definitely.

"Crawford Foster. And somebody called Butch. Butch was the double."

"Sorry. None of them mean a thing."

Well, that was that. I'd picked myself a client a jury of Communists would convict against orders from the Kremlin. I'd alienated Framboise, Martha Scaley would be sore when she found out, and all the business that paid me real money would fly away like a covey of frightened quail when it was known I'd taken on an obvious murderer.

So smart I thought I was. All I'd done was fall flat on my fat pratt.

"But there was something funny in that list," he said. "Carol Weller, you said near the first? Then later on you mentioned the name Foster. That stirred an old memory. Back in the days in Toronto, John had a girl. A very beautiful little girl. Her name was Carol Foster."

"That does it," I said gleefully. "That spills the molten solder all over the machine shop floor. Was she blonde?"

"Not that I remember. Seems to me her hair was light brown."

"That doesn't matter. Did she dance?"

"No. Not professionally, if that's what you mean."

"That doesn't matter," I said. "She could learn, couldn't she? Did she have a brother?"

"I never met her family."

"Did the Sark marry her?"

"Not as far as I know. I got the impression he didn't have to."

"I got business," I said. "All kinds of business. Sit here and be good and do just what they tell you. After you get out, come around and see me."

I left. Maybe roadrunners move faster. Maybe.

The two Homicide boys were hanging around outside the door.

"Treat him with kid gloves," I flung at them as I screamed by. "He's practically a free man."

It just shows you how cocky some people can get too soon.

Scene Thirteen

MY OFFICE WAS IN the Canam Building on Dominion Square. The Canam Building was smaller than the Dominion Square Building, which was just across the street, but it was newer.

I let myself in. It was a large single office, with a waiting room solidly partitioned off across the front. The waiting room held three chairs with dark blue leather seats, a mahogany table well sprinkled with magazines I tried to remember to change once a month, and two ashtrays on stands, all sitting on dark blue twist-tuft broadloom. In my office more dark blue broadloom, more blue-seated chairs and a mahogany desk. The whole place tried to look like the fees I sometimes got away with charging.

I sat down at the desk and turned on the phone. It was somewhat past eight o'clock and with any luck she'd still be in bed. I looked in the phone book. There was no Carol Weller there, but I remembered I'd got her number at the Caliban Club. I dug it out of my notebook and dialed it. I let her phone buzz until I got tired of counting the rings. Either she wasn't answering, or she'd skipped somewhere, or she'd been out all night and wasn't home yet. Or she was up and out somewhere, but I didn't believe that one.

No further action suggested itself immediately. I sat and thought about the link between Eddie Herbinger's cottage and the Sark's death. It had come through the fog at last. Eddie gave dope to Crawfie Foster to sell, and Crawfie had probably been Carol Weller's brother before she changed her name, Carol Weller was Matt Croll's moll, and Matt Croll had been Sark's bodyguard.

Supposing I knew who killed Sark, which I thought I did, I had no evidence and I couldn't see a good motive. Not a really good one. But the evidence and the motive were tangled up with that chain of people.

Because the Sark was taken to that island to be killed. That was the one big point I fastened on. Sark thought he was going there to hide out, but one of the people in the chain arranged that island as the hideout so advantage could be taken of its isolation to rub him out.

There were still a lot of things that didn't tie in. I didn't know why Carol had lied to me and said she met the Sark in Reno, when she'd been his lay in Toronto ten years before that. I didn't know whether Pamela fitted into it, or if so, where. I didn't know for sure who shot lame Sammy. I didn't know why the Sark had built up a pathological fear of Geysek when Geysek had no intention of hitting him for anything but a job. I didn't know how I was going to get my murderer arrested, even if I shouted his name from the corner of Peel and St. Catherine. But I had something to work on.

I went and worked on it.

I drove the Riley in third gear over to Dorchester Street – there was too much traffic for me to shift up to high – and parked in front of Louie Two's. Louie Two's had been closed for eight hours. That was the law. Louie Two's was just about as closed as a dance hall on Saturday night. I went in and sat down at a table. It was dim and reasonably cool in the barroom, and quiet. There were three ex-pugs and a lush sportswriter at one table, very beat and talkless. There was a drunk passed out with his head on his arms at another table. A few busboys were slumped along the walls, and all the waiters were sitting down. Louie Two was in front of the bar and Louie Three was behind it. That made the corporation complete. People who came there for the first time always wanted to know where Louie One was, but he was dead. He died in 1928.

Louie Two came over and sat down with me. He was bald as an osprey, kindly as rain on farmland, philosophical as a hack driver. He was the squarest crook in town.

"Halaa, Russy," he said. "Last round just coming up, on that house. I got to go home get some sleep. What'll you drink?" He waved to the waiters with his whole arm.

I shook my head and said I wasn't drinking. None of the waiters had even got to their feet. I gave Louie Two a dollar. "Here," I said. "Tear up my I.O.U."

"I already done so," he assured me. "Any time, Russy, any time."

"Thanks. Thanks for telling Creep Jones I was okay. What have I ever done for you?"

"Treated me like you liked me, not like I was a character."

"About Creep Jones," I said. "May I ask? He told me he was here Tuesday night, talking to you until one o'clock. Then he was called away. He got back here about half-past three. He wouldn't lie to me about any of that, would he? Because he knows I'm a friend of yours, and I'd come here and ask you."

"Tuesday night. That was a quiet night," Louie Two informed me. "We had to send out for steaks only once through the night. The place was filled up for a while with *schlemils* that drank just beer. Louie Three was off at the

Forum to see a wrestling match and I had to tend bar myself, but all I did was open beer bottles all night. I ..."

"About Creep Jones," I prompted.

"You're right. He wouldn't lie to you. He came in behind the bar and sat there and talked to me. He was there maybe from ten o'clock."

"And afterward?"

"He came back. Maybe three-thirty, yes."

"I want to leave a message for him. Did you see him last night?"

"Why a message? Tell him," Louie Two said. He got up and yelled, "Hey, Creepy!"

The battered bazooka of the Creep rose from behind the bar. He'd been sitting beside Louie Three.

"I'll leave you talk with him alone," Louie Two said and went behind the bar with Louie Three. Creep came bringing a glass of beer with him and sat down in the chair Louie Two had left.

"Salutations," Creep said. "Cooler, this morning."

"If you say so."

"I haven't seen Matt since I saw you."

"Find him. Tell him I want to see him."

"Sure."

"Tonight."

"No promise. I don't know where he is. I got to wait till he phones me here. Louie Two's letting me sleep here because the blueboys put an eye on my flop. Maybe tonight. No promise."

"I got your information for you. The body on the island was the Sark."

"You know?"

"That's the way I figure it."

"If you say so," he gave me back.

"That cleans Matt on your books, does it?"

"Yeah. I'm glad, too. He's okay."

"If you say so," I deadpanned. It was getting to be a bad habit with both of us.

"I used to be a truck driver. All kinds of trucks but most of them hot this way, that way. Hot trucks or hot cargo. Sark took me off that and gave me a job I could be honest at. Not that I wanted to be honest, but I was getting awful tired of being slugged with somebody holding my mitts, and skipping out of warm burgs, and sleeping in truck cabs. Sark squared with me. I'd have to work on the rat that gunned him, even if it was Matt. I'm glad it wasn't Matt."

"Why wasn't it Matt?"

"If I took the double to the lake, Sark was getting cold in his kitchen right then. Matt came out of there when we started up. He would have to have told me to make it right. Also, he would have had to told me it was Butch I was driving. If I took Butch to the lake, one of the two I drove killed Sark. But if I took Sark to the lake it's all right. Because I delivered him there safe and then me and Matt left."

"Who says Matt didn't go back and kill him? Afterward?"

"Matt says. Who says he did?"

"Nobody. But someone did."

"Yeah. We'll find out."

"Who's 'we'?"

"Matt and me. We're working on it."

"Good luck. I'm working on it too. You tell Matt that."

"We'll be around," he said.

I could have tried Carol again from there, but I remembered I'd left the phone turned on in my office. I went back there and called her apartment, and this time I counted the rings. Ten.

Carol wasn't in circulation.

If I'd only let it ring five times and then given up, I might have been all right. The way I timed it, the outside door opened before I could get away. I was too busy to see Mrs. Martha Scaley, but she was going to see me.

"Please come in," I said. "Sit down. I'm afraid I have only a few minutes. Do you mind?"

"Good morning, Russell," she said pleasantly. "You are at work early. I wouldn't expect you to keep such regular hours."

"Very regular," I said. "Seven a.m. to three a.m. Call me any time at all. If I'm asleep I have a tape-recorder you can talk to."

She didn't like the tone of my voice. I don't really blame her.

"Russell," she said, "you don't have to be on the defensive with me."

"I'm sorry," I said meekly enough. "Sometimes I forget to change gears between the different kinds of people I talk to. I didn't mean to be tough. You just said the wrong thing. Since I took this sweet little case of yours I've had about five hours' sleep, sum total, in two nights and a day."

"That is hardly my fault."

"Maybe not. But there it is, for what I can make of it."

"I did not," she said with a strong emphasis on the not, "retain your services for a murder investigation. If you chose to go off investigating murders, that is on your own head."

"Thank you," I said, somewhat bitter. "I wondered how our relationship stood. I told Martin to ask you. I thought perhaps you would not want me to investigate the Sark's murder on your behalf, since what you were mainly interested in was that Inez should be rid of the Sark. So I dug into the murder on my own, until I got another client to sponsor me."

"And who was that?"

"The man the police think killed the Sark."

"You said two days ago that all of this was out of your line of work."

"Once, just a few days ago, it was," I said.

She studied me carefully. "Now, before we end our relationship, tell me whether you found out about John Sark's first wife."

"In my wanderings I met a girl who called herself Carol Weller. She said she had knows Sark in Reno, Nevada, in 1940 or so. She said he was then in Reno getting a divorce from a Toronto girl."

"I see. It doesn't make any real difference, of course. Not now. But that is what I hired you for, so I'm glad to hear that you found out something."

"But this girl, this Carol Weller, was probably lying. So all you bought yourself was a thousand dollars' worth of nothing at all."

"Happily, I can afford it." She got up and walked to the door.

"Unless you count my saving Inez from getting arrested for murder. For murdering her husband."

Martha Scaley was a fine figure of a woman. If anything, her figure was a little finer after that remark. A little more drawn in and poised and restrained. Her elegant white hair tilted up and her chin came out. She looked at me with the violet-blue eyes as though I was something that lived at the border of a lake, just a bit below the water. But she came back and sat down again.

"Inez went out with a party on Tuesday night, the night the Sark was killed. The party got around to the Paul Archers' on the Boulevard and stayed there drinking until eleven-thirty. Then they moved on to the Trafalgar. All except Inez. She separated herself from them, said she was going to your place to get a wrap, and went to Sark's apartment instead to see if he'd come back. According to Inez she didn't even get up the nerve to leave her taxi and go up to the apartment, but I don't quite believe that. It doesn't tally with her character. If she'd made up her mind to look into the apartment, she looked in. And it was just around that time the Sark was killed. Or rather the Sark's double was killed. The Sark himself wasn't killed until three or four o'clock Wednesday morning. When Inez was supposedly in her little bed in your house, sleeping, only I expect there was no one sleeping with her so no one can swear to that. And don't give me the line about the house being all locked up."

She was a taut, white old woman. What she finally said was, "You know Inez isn't a murderess." The way she said it, it meant she was just that vital infinitesimal bit unsure.

"Yes. I know she isn't a murderess." I said it mostly to make amends, but I was pretty sure.

"And that is why you've been working on the murders? To prove Inez innocent?"

"I hope so. I haven't proved anything yet. Theoretically, I'm not representing Inez or you in connection with the murders; I'm representing an ex-convict named Albert Geysek. But I got into the thing originally because it seemed the police might fasten on Inez if they couldn't find anyone better. They have Geysek right now, but that's just a laugh. They'll have to let him go by tonight, whether I do anything or not, because it's easy to see the evidence against him is a clear and deliberate plant. Then they may start thinking about Inez again, and they may arrest her the way I thought they would before now. That's why I have to trip up the real killer."

She said woodenly, "You left a message with Martin for me. You said the thousand dollars had been used up. Of course, I'm not going to place any limit on your account now."

"It won't be more than a thousand in any case," I assured her. "It was only that I was sore at the world last night."

When she went out I tried Carol's number again, just to prove how bad my luck was, and it was still that bad.

I'd been hatless since I tangled with Matt and Creep and jumped out of Carol's window, so I got my other hat from the costumer behind the door. I liked it better anyhow. I turned my phone off so it would get answered somewhere else. I sallied.

I nosed the Riley along St. Catherine through the midmorning trams and went up Jeanne Mance to Crawford Foster's. Inside was the same bare, filthy room where the boys played their craps. It was empty now. Through a short passage, past the bathroom door on one side and the door to a little kitchen on the other, was a second room. It was the bedroom. It was just as bare, filthy and empty and it smelled worse. The only sign of Crawfie was the unmade bed he'd slept in.

I stood there and looked at the crumpled mess of dirty sheet and sleazy blanket and greasy pillowslip and behind me a siren came groaning up the street and stopped at the door. There was a pause and then a rattle of several pairs of feet skipping up the front steps. One man came on alone from there, along the outside corridor and into the from room of Crawfie's apartment. I went to meet him.

"Hello, Raoul," I said. "Your tail did a good job. I didn't suspect a thing."

Framboise looked big and broad and ugly and mad. His arms, long as a monkey's, hung at his sides a little bit curled. His hands were curled up too, tensed and waiting and itching to grab something and do it a mischief.

"Little late in the morning for you to stay on duty," I said.

He was excited. His big broad pasty face had a purple tinge and his eyes squinted at me. "All right, *bâtard*. I got you w'ere you talk to me," he bellowed.

"Nope," I said. I shook my head too, in case he missed it.

He came close to me. One hand the size of a Montreal telephone book and a lot more clinging came up and grabbed a handful of my jacket, shirt, tie and chest. He dragged me up to his face. It didn't smell of shaving lotion.

"You wen' to Louie Two's. You foun' out somet'ing t'ere t'at bring you 'ere, *correct*? W'ose place is t'is? Who you hexpec' to fin' 'ere, heh? W'at you look for, w'at you pull? *Qu'est que c'est*? Talk! Quick!"

"Let me go," I said quietly, "and calm down. Your English is all gone to hell when you're so excited."

He shoved me a little away from him and hit me on the side of the head with his fist. It wasn't much. It didn't even knock me down, because he still held my jacket with his other hand. It was only sort of like being hit on the side of the head with the flat front of a tramways bus rushing to make a traffic light.

He hit me again. This time I was expecting it. I started to get my arm up, but my ears were still trying to clap hands from the first smash and I didn't make it. He connected. My ear burst and a hot trickle of liquid ran down the side of my neck. Then my stomach was suddenly right behind my teeth and I was leaning forward on his stiff arm being sorry about all the beer and rye I'd drunk in the last few days.

"*Maudit* son of a bitch!" he gritted and dropped me.

I pulled my arms in under me and began to get up. It was like trying to lift a streetcar on your back. I pulled my knees in under my body. They were on long ropes and I had to walk around the capstan four times to reel them in. I made the big effort and heaved with my hands and ended up on my haunches with my head rolling around on my shoulders like a ball bearing in a shallow saucer.

Framboise said, "I'm sorry. *Pardon.* I los' my temper."

"Jesus and Jehovah, then go find it," I told him.

"I t'ought at leas' you would fight. I don't get some satisfaction from pounding you up if you jus' stan' t'ere."

My mouth felt numb, like the rest of my face. "I won't tell you a damn thing," I said, moving my lips stiffly.

He studied me with his squinting little eyes. He was sorry for me, but to him I was a bastard and he was still mad at me. "I give you till I come back on duty tonight," he said, "an' if you aren't aroun' t'en to tell w'at you know, I'll come look for you. W'en I fin' you I'll give you more. A lot more. I don' let anyone hol' out on me."

"Next time you see me, keep your fists up," I told him. "I won't be your punching bag twice. Okay, now I've lost mine. Keep the hell out of my hair, don't put your stoolies to trail me, and don't show up, please where I'm trying to do your work for you. When I get ready I'll give you your murderer knotted up like a stutterer's tongue."

"Tonight!" he said.

He went out and he and his two boys went down the steps. The squad car doors slammed. They went away fast, playing the siren full throat to get Framboise home to his hot breakfast.

Scene Fourteen

WHEN I CAME OUT OF THE PIC and out of the Mount Royal and the world was quieter and more placid, I thought I should go look for Carol. I thought it was lunch time. When I considered carefully, I was sure it was lunch time, and I wasn't going to work through lunch again.

The heat had largely left the city since the day before. Today there was no sun and little humidity; there was even a breeze.

At first glance the apartment didn't seem like much of a place for lunch. The only protein in the frig was eggs. While I was wondering what to do with them I heated a frying pan spit hot. I broke three eggs into the pan and scrambled them up with salt and a touch of ketchup and pepper from the mill and tarragon. I looked in the can cabinet and there was a can of Catelli's spaghetti. I dumped the spaghetti on top of the eggs and mixed well. With a glass of milk, it wasn't bad. If I ever did it again I'd remember to add a bit of Roquefort cheese and go easier on the tarragon.

I had something new. I had one small fact from Geysek. I'd sacrificed my reputation and my right ear to get it, and I hadn't done anything with it yet.

If Carol and Crawfie were linked, if say they were brother and sister, I had a complete chain from Eddie Herbinger to the Sark, I had Eddie to start, and Crawfie, Carol, Matt and Sark. Somewhere in that chain was the answer to why the Sark had been shot on Eddie's island.

Figure it this way. The Sark is afraid Geysek will come to get him. He hides out on the island, leaving the double to take the bullets. But someone gets to him on the island and bullets him too. Now, suppose one little thing. Suppose the person who suggested he go to the island did that so the Sark would get shot. This would be someone who knew about the island and knew Sark, too; that might let out Eddie and Crawfie. It would be somebody who wanted Sark killed; there was no obvious reason why any of them wanted Sark killed.

Unless…

"Get me Toronto," I told the telephone.

What particular part of Toronto, the girl wanted to know. So I told her, and she got me Talbot Gray.

"Tabby," I said, "I have a job for you that I don't know how you can do, but can you find old marriage license records?"

"Hell! Russ!" he yacked. "How are you? When you coming up this way again? How's business?"

"Fine," I said, "no sooner than I can help, and fine. And old marriages. About twenty years old. Can you find?"

"Sure," he said, all legal and business. "Whose marriage?"

"John Sark. I think his name was John Sark then. And Carol Foster. I hope her name was Carol Foster then."

"I'll find it," he told me, "if you're right on one of them. What's it all about?"

"Bigamy. Motive for murder. Greed."

"Greed," he said. "That reminds me. Fifty dollars."

"Send me a bill. I feel generous. Find the marriage and it'll be a hundred. Find it today for two hundred."

"Where's my hat?" he said, and hung up.

So that was it: maybe.

Carol could be Sark's first wife, if the anonymous letter sent to Martha Scaley was right and Sark had had a first wife. Everybody kept saying Carol and Sark hadn't married, and Carol had her own story about his getting a Reno divorce from someone else, but that story sounded like so much bushwah.

Carol could be his first wife he hadn't bothered to divorce, or hadn't divorced properly, which would make her still his legal wife. And legal wives inherit a lot of money, no matter what, in Quebec. Even if they're neglected in the will they can apply for their cut, and if a man dies intestate they get everything except the Provincial and Federal Governments' fractions.

I wished I knew about the will. I wished I hadn't made Raoul Framboise mad at me so I couldn't find out about things like that. But it didn't matter too much, because will or no will, Carol would be in the chips if she was really Carol Sark.

There were other things I wished I could get Framboise to tell me. Maybe even if he wouldn't talk to me he would tell them to someone else. I put the dirty dishes in the sink and went down for Riley.

MacArnold lived in a one-room apartment in an old converted house on Shuter Street, above Milton. He lived there, meaning he kept his beer there and he slept there. He slept there most of the day. He was sleeping there when I arrived. I hammered on his door until he stopped sleeping.

He said, "Come in, and don't stay. I spend my free time writing novels."

I came in. I went to his kitchen and got myself a beer. I said, "Everybody has to do something with his spare time. Some people go to movies. Some play canasta. You write novels. I get drunk." I drank some beer.

"I get drunk while I write novels," MacArnold sail.

"Don't think I'm interested, but what kind?"

"Realistic."

"Of course."

"Realism cast in a mould. Caught in a structure. The structure of a classical tragedy, fault not in our stars, man his own destruction."

"Appropriate to yesterday," I said.

"Eternally appropriate."

"No. The world is a bigger mess than Sophocles' or Shakespeare's. Their men could act and accomplish, or waver and be lost. Now men can act and the system is too big for them to accomplish, or they can waver and nothing much happens."

"You came here. You want something?"

"Oh, that. I just want sympathy."

"Why?"

"I 'ave cut my t'roat wit' Framboise. He told me so himself."

"How come?"

I told him about Geysek. I told him about Geysek's gun and what it had done. I told him about taking Geysek on as a client, though I didn't say why I'd done it or how I knew someone else was guilty.

"You're a muddler. You're a goddamned idiot."

"I know." I wasn't going to be proud. Not yet.

"For a P.I. you're awful young and naïve and cocky. I could teach you a lot about the racket."

"You could teach me a lot about murder. I haven't had it mixed up in my business before."

"Your business has been a soft touch."

"Sure," I said. I went out and found another beer, but I was slowing down. I came back.

"You were right," I said, "I want something."

He didn't answer right away. Whatever I wanted, if it was only a penny to weigh myself, he wasn't sure he'd give. He was sore because I made ten times what he did for knowing less. I had been brought up in Westmount and sent to a private school and supported through McGill and graduated into a business that was a soft touch. He'd graduated from high school into a job that didn't buy him enough of anything, even beer.

I believed in heavy inheritance taxes, but I couldn't expect him to know that.

"In your novel, I'm a bum," I guessed. "But we can agree on one thing. We don't like murder. This murder was triplets: Sammy, Butch, and Sark. It could spread. I want to stop it."

"Then why not just let Geysek get swung for it."

"Because he didn't do it. He couldn't have done it. I know who did. I just want proof."

"Proof against whom?"

"I get proof, you get another exclusive."

"All right. Fair enough. But why did you make Framboise sore at you? He could be more help to you than anyone else. He's cops, and murder is his business. Why couldn't you just string along and just try to help him or even lead him, instead of making him look like an asshole?"

"Proof, looking for proof. I thought Geysek could tell me something if I got close enough to him. He told me a little."

"All right, what do you want?"

"Worry Framboise for me, will you? After he comes

back on duty tonight. Not much. Not enough to get yourself in Dutch. Just enough to make him see Geysek didn't do it."

"How?"

"When was the little gimp Sammy killed?"

"Probably around nine on Tuesday."

"Yes, and the way I heard it they know he wasn't shot later than nine. And Geysek's train came in at ten-thirty. See what I mean? Sammy's murder and Butch's murder were set up to look as though Geysek did them. That was the plant against him. But the killer made a slip; maybe thought Geysek took an earlier train. Suggest that to Framboise. Suggest he might check the bullet that killed Sammy against the gun they found with Geysek. I have a theory, and the theory says Sam's executioner came from the gun that killed Butch and Sark. The gun planted with Geysek."

He asked me, "How does this help lay the killer, that gets me my exclusive?"

"It doesn't. It's the favor to me that gets Geysek out of chains, and that gets you your exclusive. When I trip the killer. Or when Framboise shakes the inertia out of his entrails and goes looking for him, which he will do when he loses Geysek as a suspect."

"Okay," MacArnold said. "What the hell? I'll try it. I hope you're right, though. I hope the bullet matches."

"It will," I promised him. "Another thing. Enlarge on the Sark for me, will you?"

"What about him? Name the angle. I could fill a book."

"Briefly, his business."

"Nightclubs, mainly the Spadina. Gambling clubs outside the city limits. No names for them, but I can give you some addresses. Not much else, in the last few years. He was in a lot of other things, but he gradually cleaned himself up while he was going respectable."

"His set-up, his organization?"

"Managers for the gambling clubs and the night clubs, except the Spadina. He managed that himself. Sammy, who probably kept the books for the whole empire. Two hoods who trailed him around, one to drive his car and one to look out the back window. And the double, but I didn't know about him until the killings."

"Enlarge on the hoods," I requested.

"The car driver, small and aged and beat-up. Quiet, peaceful little character with an old wife somewhere in the city. Louie Two says she's a good cook, so he goes home to eat. The rest of the time he hangs out at Louie Two's when he's not working."

"Creep Jones."

"Why ask me about him if you've met him? The other hood is Matt Croll. Met him?"

"I have," I grunted. "Watch me when I walk out. The limp is from Matt. What's with him?"

"Crafty. I think he did most of the general managing of the gambling set-up, under Sark, and he was around the Spadina a lot, too. I have an idea Sark hired him just for a gun, but he moved a little higher than that. The boys say he came from St. Louis, and they say St. Louis would like to see him come home – in shackles. He carries a nice long knife to use where a gun would make too much noise, and from time to time unimportant little characters have been found in dim places, kind of carved up. They never pinned anything on Matt. He's gone respectable, like the Sark, in a sort of a way. Has an apartment on Peel above Sherbrooke that an interior decorator charged him plenty to fix up. He got the place about six months ago and shortly afterward he got a well-preserved blonde for furniture."

"I wonder where he found the blonde?"

"Maybe she came from St. Louis. Who knows? She hadn't been around before that."

"Good enough," I said. "Well, happy writing. Don't forget about Framboise, tonight." I drained my glass and got up.

Scene Fifteen

I KNEW WHERE Crawfie Foster's studio was.

It was on St. François-Xavier, which is the second street below St. James, and it was just west of Hospital Street. It was a small, narrow-fronted old yellow building of rough stucco. I knew it was there and I could even see it, but I couldn't get to it. The lower part of Montreal, the old business and financial district on the flats just above the river, was built before automobiles were invented. Some people swear it must have been built before carriages were invented. The streets were made wide enough for two men on horseback to pass, but carriages would have a hard time. Cars had a harder time, and if there were trucks around the whole thing became impossible. I cruised around the narrow streets. I crossed St. François-Xavier three times, and each time it was impossible to turn onto it. I gave up and took the Riley all the way back to Craig Street before I found a parking space.

The old yellow stucco building had scooped-out stone steps, a door that had been repainted without scraping until the paint was about as thick as the wood, and a wide corridor that had all the hush and dark and awesomeness of a morgue vault. I got to the end of the corridor and started up a set of ancient wooden stairs, dingy as lignite and worn as an old woman's rosary. They went up, turned at a landing, and went on up to the second floor. When you got past the landing you couldn't see the corridor below.

When I got past the landing, I heard the downstairs door close softly, but with a twanging *click*.

Ten cold, furry little mice with sharp feet crawled up my back underneath my shirt, and when they got to my collar ten more started from away down my back and they went all the way up too.

If Framboise still had a tail on me he wouldn't come into the building. He'd park across the street behind a copy of *La Presse* and wait for me to come out. This wasn't a tail Framboise had on me. This was a tail of a different horse.

There wasn't any way out except the front door. The lower corridor was darker than the 1,750-foot level of the Sullivan mine. I wasn't armed, my skull was soft as anyone else's, and I didn't want to get hit on the ear again either. Suddenly I felt I'd like company, lots of company. I got to the second floor and found Crawfie's name on the third door to the left. I went in.

It was a small, square room and it was deserted. About half the room was filled with the biggest, oldest rotary dryer in use on this continent.

I closed the door behind me and I was careful not to turn my back to it. I looked over the rest of the office. The plain wooden chairs. A desk littered with prints and paste-ups and artwork and old plate holders, and sitting in the middle where Crawfie'd laid it down, an unloaded Speed Graphic.

There was a door in the middle of the far wall. A solid wooden door. I went to it and tried the knob. It wasn't locked. I got the door about six inches open and saw darkness and a dim eerie green light when a yell split the air.

"Close the goddamn door," Crawfie yelled. "You'll

ruin these films, you fool!"

I paid attention to that like Junior pays attention to Mommy's voice, when she can't see him. I opened the door all the way. I felt beside it for a light switch and flooded the darkroom with yellow brightness. The gush of light froze an animal snarl on Crawfie's comic face. His mouth was open ,ready to yell some more, but he saw who it was and didn't yell. His mouth slowly closed.

I came in and shut the door. I stood myself to the left of the door so if anyone else came in I'd be behind it when it opened. I didn't wish Crawfie any hard luck, but supposing someone in a shooting mood opened the door I'd sooner have him shoot Foster than Teed.

Crawfie was in shirt and pants with an old acid-eaten khaki lap apron tied around his fat stubby trunk. His heavy horn rims were so dirty and splattered they must have fogged the world for him. His flabby slack-jawed face was a dirty white color. He stood there without moving, waiting to see what I'd do. He was scared.

"Relax," I said, "I didn't bring the Mounties with me."

He took off his glasses and wiped his eyes with the back of his hand. He looked as if he was going to cry. Maybe he thought I'd forgotten about him and would never come back.

"I want you to talk to me. I want you to start when you were born and tell me all about yourself. And I don't want any more lies, like the story that you never knew Sark. Okay. Start."

He got the idea.

"I was born in Toronto," he stuttered, "in 1914. I went to school there and worked for a photographer, when I finished high school. I came to Montreal in 1941. I ..."

"Brothers and sisters?"

"I had one sister. Three years older."

"Name?"

"Carol." He waited for me to ask another question.

"You aren't filling in detail. Tell me more about your family."

"My mother died in 1937. My father left Toronto and disappeared, before that, and I was supporting my mother five or six years before she died. Carol didn't help. We used to hear from her once in a while. She was a dancer, in night clubs, mostly in different cities in the States. She never settled down in one place very long."

"When'd you last hear from her?"

"Oh, maybe five years ago."

I went over to him and hit him across the face with the back of my hand. He hadn't put his glasses back on and my hand hit his eyes. I hurt him. I went back and stood where I had been before with my back against the wall beside the door.

"What was that for, Teed?" he whined.

"Telling fibs. All right, I'm tired of talking about your sister Carol. Let's talk about Carol Weller instead."

That made him cry. He blubbered, "I was only trying to keep her out of it. I didn't want her linked to me if I'm going to get hauled up for doping. Honest, Teed, she isn't anyone you're interested in. She isn't doping, she's only seen me twice since she came to Montreal. Once she came here and surprised me. I hadn't seen her for ten years. I was glad to see her. I offered her money, but she said she was doing all right. She had a job dancing at the Caliban and she had a boyfriend who wanted to marry her."

"She'd been divorced from the Sark, I suppose. So she could marry this guy if she wanted to."

"She never married the Sark. Sure, she went out with

him a lot back in Toronto, but she didn't marry him.

"Who was the new boyfriend, here in Montreal?"

"She didn't say. She said she was using his apartment, but that was all right, because he had a hotel suite where he stayed."

"And she wouldn't take your money."

His mouth pulled down in a bitter sulky line. "Not then. Later she wanted some. That's my family for you. My old man runs away and leaves me with Mother. He even wrote me and said it wasn't any use for me to try tracing him, he'd changed his name. And Carol, as soon as Carol gets the idea I'm in the chips she wants some. That's how I saw her the second time. I was doing some work for Eddie – you know, with the stuff. I started up north to take some junk to the island. I started before dark, that was my mistake. She must have been tailing me for days. She followed me all the way to the lake. It was dark then, but she crawled right up behind me in her car, and when I got into the boat with the suitcase she turned her car lights on me. She came down to the boat laughing like hell and said she'd followed me just for a gag, and what was I doing? I didn't tell her much."

"But you told her something. You would."

"I said the cottage on the lake was mine. I said I was in a racket running hot American money out of the country, and this was a pickup spot. Then she wanted a cut and I told her I could giver her one grand to shut up, but it wasn't worth any more. She said she'd come see me and get it, but she never did. She just called me after that and said she'd be needing to use my island for a while, and I was to make sure no one went up there. I was to stall my racket off until she gave me the sign. I said I couldn't do that, I was only a little boy in the set-up and they wouldn't do it for me. So she said to tell them Sark wanted the island for a while for a hideout."

"Which means she was back with the Sark again, after all the years since Toronto."

"That's what I thought. I thought maybe the Sark was the man who'd given her the apartment. But she never said so. She never said any more than that."

"When did she want the island?"

"This week. Beginning Monday, until she gave the all-clear."

"And she never asked for her cut from you?"

"No. She never mentioned it when she called. And I sure as hell didn't. I gave Eddie a story. I told him Mortland had met me at the island on my last trip and told me some heat was on, and we were to lay low, let it cool off this week and not shove anything through. We were just to sit on any stuff that came in and wait."

"If Eddie had called Mortland you'd have been in a poor spot. You daren't dare a risk like that."

"It wasn't a risk," he said. "Eddie and Mortland communicate only one way. They leave notes for each other on the island. I take the notes Eddie writes up there, and I bring Mortland's back to him. I was going to go up when Carol gave me an okay, and I'd have opened Mortland's note and read it and doctored it. Ditto with anything Eddie wrote."

"It was still a risk. Suppose you weren't the one to make the next trip. Suppose Eddie sent Pamela up with some stuff."

"Her?" he squeaked, surprised. "She never had anything to do with the racket. She never went up there."

"You're wrong. She went up there with stuff the night the Sark was killed."

"Oh, my God!" His eyes widened. "Then she knew. I was more afraid of her than I was of Eddie. Eddie wasn't going to tumble that I'd agreed with Carol to let Sark have the island. I had that angle taken care of. But Pam could have found out. She must have known. Eddie never would have sent a load of junk up to the island after I warned him off, and if he was going to he would have gone himself. She wasn't taking junk up there. She'd found out about Sark being there, from knowing ... "

He stopped dead, because the door opened.

Nobody came in. The knob was twisted and the door was pushed hard and it swung back on me. I couldn't see a thing. But Crawfie was seeing something, something that made his eyes spring wide until the whites showed above the irises and the big sloppy mouth drop foolishly open and his breath draw in fast and sobbing.

Then he screamed. He screamed like a woman in a falling elevator. And simultaneously with the scream came the pop of a gun, a small gun because it wasn't a big noise even in that confined space.

The bullet hit him all right. It shoved him sideways against the bench behind him, and his hands clutched at that as he tried to stay on his feet. Then his legs went liquid and he fell in a heap on the floor.

I heard footsteps, a man's footsteps, running to the outer door. The door opened and then slammed. Very respectfully I stuck my head around the darkroom door. The outer office was empty. The gunman had known I was there, because he had been in the outer office listening to Crawfie and me talk. But he hadn't waited to ambush me. Listening carefully I could hear his feet beating down the stairs. I went to Crawfie and laid him out neatly on his back. He was passed out, but by no means dead. I pulled the bib of the lab apron aside and ripped his shirt open. The bullet had got into his chest about two inches above the left nipple. It had hit at an angle and come out through his armpit. His pectoral muscle was probably a bit ripped up, and he wouldn't be raising that arm above his head for a while, but he wasn't dying. He wasn't even losing much blood. He wasn't in shock, he'd just passed out from fright.

I left him there and went to the outer office. I phoned Dr. Danny Moore's office and Danny answered. "I got business for you," I told him. "It pays to have friends like me."

"What is it?"

"Just a dirty little gunshot wound."

"You sound okay," he said. "Sit down and take a neat drink and wait for me."

"No, no, not me. A business associate."

"Your business is rougher than it used to be."

I rubbed the ear Framboise had worked on. "I know," I said. I gave him the number on St. François-Xavier. "Come on over, will you? The guy isn't dying, but he could stand some attention. I've got to go find the gunner, if I can. After you tape the lug up you'd better call in the law."

"Call the law yourself," he said, and hung up.

I got a print from Crawfie's desk and wrote on the back, "*You* call the cops. I didn't." I took it in and laid it on Crawfie. He was a healthier color than he had been since he saw the gun pointing at him.

I went through the outer office and into the corridor. Quite a crowd had gathered out there. An elderly citizen with a green eye-shade, in shirt sleeves and an unbuttoned vest, a scrawny kid with ink on his fingers and a drafting pen in his hand, and two old stenos of the type you engage when they're young and ugly so they won't distract your boys, and then you have to keep them the rest of their lives because no one marries them.

The elderly citizen said, "Was that a shot?"

"Sure," I told him, "you might go in and stand over Mr. Foster. There's a doctor coming."

He looked at me suspiciously. I opened my coat and showed him I had no gun. "The man who fired the shot ran out," I said. "You didn't see him, did you?"

"Nah," he said. "I had to put down the phone before I came out to the corridor."

"Nah," said the draftsman. The stenos shook their heads.

I turned and went down the stairs. As long as I could see them they were still standing there watching me. It was lucky for Crawfie he didn't need a tourniquet.

Maybe I was lucky, too. Maybe my luck was beginning to get better. A big green truck was parked just beside the front door of the building. The cab door on the curb side was open as though the driver's assistant had gone to make a delivery. The driver himself was sitting in the cab.

"Hey!" I called.

He opened his eyes. They were red-rimmed, watery, hungover eyes. "Uh?" he said.

"Did someone just come running out of this building?"

"Uh?"

"How would you like a big glass of beer, lots of foam, with lumps of greasy pork fat floating around in it?"

"Uh?" Then the words penetrated. He wrinkled his nose. "Ugh!" he said. I left him.

I went back to the Ticker Tape Tavern. I sat down at the same table I'd had before. I ordered two glasses of draft again. The same waiter brought them. "I was here a few minutes ago," I told him.

He was a big man with a broken nose and alert eyes. He was English. "Yeah," he said. "You were in a while back and you drank two glasses and scrammed. I remember. I got a good memory. So what?"

I got out my wallet and let him see purple – purple for a Bank of Canada ten note. "A real good memory, eh?"

He looked at the ten carefully, not without greed, not without suspicion. "What's the play?" he asked. "Those things aren't giveaway for a joke. What you want me to remember?"

"Somebody followed me out of here when I was in before. I didn't see him. I managed to lose him. I think maybe he's trying to serve a paper on me. All I want to know is what he looks like."

He thought hard. His sharp eyes glinted and his flattened nose seemed broader as he screwed up his face.

"Yeah," he said after a minute. "Yeah, that was probably it. A little guy over at that table in the corner. I didn't serve him. I didn't see him go out either. But right after you left I noticed he was gone. The funny thing was, he left two full glasses of suds on his table. So likely he followed you."

I gave him the ten. "Good enough. That sounds like the right lead. What did he look like?"

"He was a little guy with white hair."

"You got to do better than that," I told him.

"How can I? How did I know anyone was goin' to ask me about him? Besides, I didn't even serve him. I just noticed him from across the room, like, sitting alone in the corner. He didn't have a hat on, that's how I know he had white hair. He was small and old, like, and he had on a dark blue suit. He might have been a clerk or a customers' man or even a broker. He looked neat."

"Was he plump, or thin?"

"I wouldn't be sure. I didn't see him standing."

"Okay," I said. "Thanks."

"Thank *you*." He went away. I drank my beer.

There were three men in this case with hair light enough that it might have looked white in this dim tavern. Creep Jones, Eddie Herbinger, and Martin Froste. Any one of them might have shot Crawfie Foster. That's all I could make of it.

But in the meantime I did have one hunch, and I was going to play it.

Scene Sixteen

I ZOOMED STRAIGHT over the backbone of the city in Riley, riding Victoria Avenue from Sherbrooke up through Westmount and down the other side to Cote Ste. Catherine Road. I turned right and went two blocks and parked the roadster in front of a square, red-brick apartment building labeled 4050, across the street from Eddie Herbinger's store.

I got out of Riley and crossed the street to Eddie's. I thought about how much he'd changed since I'd been there before. Then as far as I was concerned he was just a pleasant old druggist who happened to own the shack where Sark was shot, and whose niece had unluckily chosen the morning of the shooting to go fishing. A little druggist who kept large quantities of heroin in his safe because he supplied a private hospital with the stuff.

The heroin was the key. Press the key and the whole filthy sub-plot came out. The heroin led me to the dirtiest little slob in the city – an employee of Eddie's. Then I came back to the girl Pamela, and she hadn't been going fishing; she'd been delivering dope. And here I was back at Eddie – Eddie the doper....

Eddie, who was probably the basic source of supply for most of the addicts in the city. I'd seen some of those addicts. I'd been down on St. Catherine Street by Clark in back holes that smelt like unflushed toilets, looking for men who'd disappeared months, maybe even years before. Sometimes I'd found them, too, but I'd never brought one back. They weren't men at all when they'd been there a while taking the stuff. They were like the old wrecks that float in the Sargasso Sea; all stove in, covered with slime and parasitic growth, circling endlessly and uselessly in decreasing circles toward a vanishing point. It was not nice to think humans could get like that. It was not nice to think of having anything to do with somebody who helped them.

But I had to see Eddie. I had to see him because he had known the Sark was coming to his island. He knew who sent the Sark there. He maybe even knew why the Sark was shot. And for my money, Eddie had probably pulled a trigger down on St. François-Xavier Street just a few minutes back, to keep his bumboy Foster from telling me too much. Eddie had a bigger interest in all this than just protecting his dope hideout.

I kept coming back to Carol. Maybe Carol hadn't shot the Sark, but she had arranged his hide-out. If she was Sark's first wife, she stood to get a big bite of moolah from his estate.

I went through the drugstore, past the pennyworth pigments and pastes in their dollarworth bottles on the left, and the sticky syrups and soda water on the right, past the deadpan fountain girl and the pimply soda jerk, past the curtain into Eddie's nineteenth century dispensary. And Herbinger was there. Alone.

He was still a nice, dignified, plump, white-haired, ruddy-skinned old man. But his white hair was hoary with unrequited sins and his ruddy skin was a reflection of hellfire.

"You made a mistake, Herbinger," I told him bluntly.

"You didn't kill Crawfie. You should have waited to make sure."

He looked at me steadily. He didn't say anything. But he wasn't afraid of me. There was almost scorn in his face.

"While you were at it, why didn't you try for me? I was right behind the door. You knew I was there, you heard me talking to Crawfie. And I've found out a lot. I've found out way too much for your good."

Then I saw the gun.

All he had to do was lift it and fire at me. But I was less than eight feet away from him and I could duck under its muzzle and throw myself at his chair. I'd probably bruise myself in a few places and the bullet might make a nasty crease through my buttock. It wouldn't do much more. I wasn't afraid of it, not a lot. But I took a deep breath and tensed and crouched a little as I narrowed the distance between us.

I wouldn't have touched him except for the gun.

As I got close to him he was still looking steadily at me and I at him. His hand hadn't moved; the gun hung useless as a broken toy in his relaxed hand. The safety was off and his finger was inside the trigger-guard but barely touching the trigger. I smashed it out of his hand and it rattled to the floor without going off.

I looked at him. I couldn't look at him any longer without doing something about it. I hit him full force across the cheek with the back of my hand. Four white streaks from my fingers and four white knots from my knuckles showed on his red face. His expression didn't change, but I felt better. I hit him again and his teeth cut his lips, and little stringers of blood appeared hesitantly at the side of his mouth and wound down into the fine white stubble on his clean little chin. But he still wasn't afraid of me.

"You've been making a lot of mistakes," I told him.

"You told me that was diamorphine in the little white boxes. I'd seen those boxes before. I'd seen them in the apartment of a yellow little bastard who couldn't keep a secret from a high school boy. I found out about you, a lot, since I was here last."

He didn't care what I said. He wasn't listening.

"Why did you shoot him? What more could he tell me that I didn't know?"

He parted his bruised lips. There was blood staining his white teeth, running red around their edges. "You know everything," he said. His voice was a strong whisper, hushed but firm. It contained no emotion. "Somebody was bound to find out everything, sooner or later. I was only waiting for the time."

"Why did you shoot Foster?"

"So he isn't dead?" the colorless whisper asked. "God must prefer to have him live and sin a while longer, that his punishment be more extreme. I was mistaken. I thought God would want him to die."

"And had appointed you his executioner?"

"Who better? Who knew more of his foulness than a man himself so foul?"

He wasn't talking to me when he spoke again. He wasn't talking to anyone, unless he was making an interim report to God. "I never wanted this," he said. "I was a little man, and people shoved me here and shoved me there. But there were things they could not make me do. They could not make me betray the profession I had chosen. And when it came to a climax, all those years ago, someone I loved was in their power. I took the only way out."

I found myself whispering, swinging into his mood despite myself. "So you poisoned him. You poisoned the Sark."

"I loved her so! She was only a child, and she had married him. He was evil, the only entirely evil man I ever found. She didn't know what he was doing to me, didn't know that the only reason he married her was to bring me into his power. Yes, I have made mistakes. I tried to poison him and failed. That was my worst mistake. He had me jailed and left her."

"Sure, that was the way it was," I prompted. "It wasn't in Hamilton; it was in Toronto, ten years ago. The Sark wanted to make some money from drug addicts. He needed a druggist to be his retail man. And you were in love with Carol. Beautiful Carol."

He went on, "I came out of jail an evil thing. I had no will left in me to say 'No.' What I have done since was within me then. I wanted to be rich and powerful, no matter how, until someday I could ruin him. No matter how. There was no virtue in life if a man like Sark could do what he had done and become what he had become. There was no sense to morals or pity or charity. There was sense only in self and in revenge."

"And so you found Mortland. You offered yourself to Mortland. And finally, Carol came back. Now she wanted revenge, too. Accidentally, through Crawfie, she stumbled on the idea of using you in her revenge. Then you explored her scheme and saw that you could help her."

For the first time he seemed to recognize my presence, to see how his thoughts were being led. For the first time, he protested. "No. I knew nothing of Sark's death until after it had been accomplished. But, oh, I was glad. As glad as though I had done it."

"What more would Crawfie have told me? What is the further link?"

He didn't answer. He was dreaming again, wordlessly now.

I looked around the old dispensary. In here it seemed more real than the glaring modern decor outside.

Maybe he was telling the truth now. Maybe he was a doper because of Sark and Carol, but no killer. He wanted Sark killed, but so did Carol, and she could have made independent plans. The choice of Herbinger's island might have been as accidental as Crawfie claimed. There might be no further tie-up.

Eddie couldn't have worked on the Sark to build him up for murder. That had to be someone the Sark knew and trusted. Someone who could whisper in his ear that Geysek was coming to get him – whisper until he was nearly crazy from fright. Until he was ready to accept any scheme offering safety. That was how the Sark was spirited away from the city and from the path of a Geysek who wanted only a job from him. That was how Sark was set up to get a hole in his head, on a quiet island where gunshots echoed only among tongueless lakes and taciturn trees.

Someone had frightened Sark. Carol had found a place for him to die when he fell for the plan. And the person who killed him had worked for her, to her advantage, on her orders. She was guilty as hell. Guilty as if she had been going around pulling triggers.

She had been married to Sark, Eddie said. She had been deserted by him when her usefulness was over. She had that score to settle with him – and his estate to claim. She had motive and she followed him to Montreal after the long years and plucked him from the breast of Westmount when she found opportunity.

All I had to do was prove it.

I looked at Eddie again. The white marks of my hand had gone from his cheek. The little trickles of blood had dried on his chin. He dreamed his wordless, sour dreams.

I stooped and took his gun from the floor. It was a light little thing. I dropped it in my jacket pocket.

I left him to all his thoughts of death.

Scene Seventeen

I WENT BACK to Sherbrooke Street and drove Riley east. The street was broad and tree-clad, the heavy green of the trees tiredly overhanging, limp after the long heat wave. It was cooler today, but with no breeze now in the afternoon.

I parked Riley up near the top of Peel, walked back to an alley, and got behind Carol's place. I kept hidden while I looked over her back fence into the yard. I remembered the yard very well. It was sodded with a particular type of hard grass that bruised you when you fell on it. I still had all the bruises.

It was a dull afternoon, without sun. If anyone was at home at Carol's, some lights should be on. But the shades were up behind the windows of her apartment, and no light came out. There was darkness behind the windows and perhaps someone was there, but it was worth taking a chance. Leaning against the yard fence was a rickety ladder that would serve my purpose. I opened the gate and went into the yard, got the ladder and leaned it against the porch roof I'd rolled from the day before. Up above, the screen I'd torn to bits in my jump stood out raggedly, like pieces of a burst sieve.

A thousand windows gaped at me from every side. There were houses to right and left and across the alley behind. Two thousand eyes could be watching me, two thousand more or less idle eyes besides the important few eyes that might be looking down from Carol's rooms.

I pretended to myself that those idle eyes were watching the repairman come to fix Carol's screen. For protective color I became the repairman. I placed the ladder and eased it into a solid position and tested it carefully, taking plenty of time, the way a repairman would. I thought like a repairman would, all the way through. I hoped I looked like a repairman.

I went up the ladder to the porch roof and across the roof to the torn screen. I looked at it sadly and shook my head in disgust. I took one of the torn pieces in my hand and examined it. If you were watching, you could almost hear me cursing at it and wondering what was the best way to fix it. I hoped the watching eyes couldn't tell I was carefully inspecting the inside of the apartment.

There was nobody in Carol's expensive living room. It was dim without lights. The crazy-patterned dark modern tables were shapeless hulks and the upholstered furniture was a series of great grey bulges. The floor with its heavy rug was dark as a shaded pool.

Then I had luck. The telephone rang. After it had rung twice, Carol came into the entry from her bedroom and answered it. I could see her in the entry, just barely. She didn't turn on any light. I kept to the edge of the window where she wouldn't notice me if she turned her head, but I pressed closer and stared harder, wishing my eyes would get accustomed to the darkness.

Set out to be a Peeping Tom, and you begin to find it might be an interesting profession.

Carol was nude. She had just come from a bath; she carried a big towel in her hand, and threw it down on a chair as she talked to the phone. Her pale yellow hair was fluffed from the steam and stood out like a crown about her face.

The window sash was open a few inches, enough for me to catch what she was saying.

"Yes, I was out all morning on that…Well, I only got in an hour ago and you rang while I was in the bath. Why didn't you have an extension put in there if you're so anxious to talk to me?…Oh. Sure. Sure thing. All right, come here. About ten minutes."

She hung up the phone. She turned on the light in the entry with a lazy, graceful gesture of her long curved arm. Then she turned toward my window, raised her arms over her head and stretched a long, relaxed, easy stretch. Her widely separated breasts didn't flatten out as she raised her arms and flexed her body. They only rode higher on her beautiful form, swelling out straight before her.

I was inexpressibly sorry the case was developing the way it was. Under any other circumstances I would have gone right through that window then, brushing the glass aside like a silk curtain with one hand. But I had to crouch there and watch her relax and turn and walk slowly back to her bedroom.

When I was entirely back to normal and my blood was running with corpuscles again instead of pure adrenalin, I resumed my repairman character. I climbed carefully down the ladder and went back to Riley for implements. I got a hammer and a pair of pliers from the trunk. Then I returned to my post and started to worry the ragged edge of the burst screen with the pliers. I sat down on the roof and pulled the screen down with me away from the window, so I wouldn't be visible from inside the apartment unless someone came right to the window and looked out.

Nobody was likely to see me, but I couldn't see inside. The buzzer sounded briefly. There was the clacking of high-heeled pumps across an uncarpeted floor, probably in the entry. The door was opened. Carol's voice came to me from a distance, as it had before, thin and a little harsh, strained through two inches of open window.

"Hi, Darling."

There was no answer. If she'd gone to the door in the same attire she'd shown me a few minutes before, I could imagine what was going on. I could have been right, because somebody came over to my window and pulled the shade all the way down. They didn't close the sash, though.

After a long time, a man sighed, it was a deep, happy sigh of complete contentment. It made me feel just dandy.

Then a heavy, rough voice without any particular accent said, "Well, Baby, did you get it?"

"Sure, Matt. It's right there in my purse. All set to go."

"Everything's working out swell."

"Sure is. After a few days, when all the fuss dies down."

"Sure, sure. But we won't rush it. No sense taking chances."

"I like to hear you say that," she told him caressingly. "It makes me sure you really love me."

"You're so right, Baby. We'll take it easy. I got business to do the next little while, anyway."

"What business?"

"The Sark was too soft. If I take over from him I only use his operations for a start. The Sark was trying to be respectable and it cramped him. We got that over him. We don't want to be society. It's a horse laugh in this crappy town. We're going to be big stuff all over the States – New York, Miami, Hollywood, anywhere we want to travel. For that, we work this town ways Sark never dared to. Ways he never even thought of."

"You got big ideas," she said. Nice girl. You could see she was proud of him.

"I can manage the Spadina and the money clubs in my lunch hour. They bring in small change. But the guy who runs them is the logical guy for a job that's been vacant for a while. The job of running Montreal. The numbers games, the slots, the blind pigs. I just have to raise my hand to the lugs in those rackets, now the Sark's gone and I'm where he used to be.

"Ah, Matt," she said, "I love it when you talk like that. It makes me feel good I was smart enough to hitch up with ..."

She stopped without finishing her sentence. It gave me a creepy feeling of foreboding, because I couldn't see what she'd seen, nor hear what she'd heard to stop her.

Matt kept quiet, too. They were both waiting for something.

Then I heard it. Somebody was opening the door of the apartment. The latch clicked as a key pulled it back, and then snapped free as the door swung wide. I imagined Matt's hand sneaking to his pocket for that big shiv.

There was a large bunch of silence. Whoever it was at the door should be right in the room with them now, but nobody was saying anything.

Then a voice spoke, it was a voice familiar to me, a soft feminine voice, not Carol's but the voice of some woman I knew. The voice when it spoke was overlaid by bitter emotion.

"Pardon me. I didn't mean to intrude," it said.

I couldn't identify it from that. Wait until she spoke again.

Matt said, "Why, Baby, I ..."

And at that instant somebody on the ground behind

me yelled, "Hey, what goes on here? What the hell you doin' up there, you?"

I was in a poor spot.

I turned around fast and started down the ladder, front side out. Behind me I heard the window shade snap up.

I wanted like all hell to turn and look back. The identity of the woman who had just come in was right on the tip of my mind, and it was driving me crazy trying to place her. But if I didn't turn, there was a chance I wouldn't be recognized.

The man who had yelled at me was an old arthritic crock in shapeless pants held up by the broadest, reddest braces in the world, which marched up over an old collarless white shirt and tried to take your attention off how filthy the shirt was. He had a face that would make a prune feel youthful, and maybe two or three teeth.

"I was fixing that screen," I told him, "It's burst."

"Yeah? Maybe you were lookin' for a good window to climb through, too. I oughta call the cops. Now get the hell out of here."

I got the hell out of there.

Scene Eighteen

When I came back to the apartment my first idea was to sit down with a cold quart of Dow and think it all over. My second idea was to sleep for a few hours. I liked the second idea better. There was nothing I could do for a while, and I was too sleepy to think. I set the alarm for six and kicked off my shoes and took to my bed under a blanket. When the alarm woke me up I felt almost *homo sapiens* again. I dragged into the bathroom and ran a full tub of water as hot as my bruised backside would stand, and after I had eased myself into the wet heat I lay back and thought.

I thought for a while with my eyes closed, but that way all I tuned in was four Sarks in four colors, one nude blonde, with her arms stretched over her head, and one surprised brunette in wet white nylon pants. To come up with anything more I had to open my eyes.

The conversation between Carol and Matt had told me a bit. Or, at least, it had confirmed some things I suspected. It confirmed Matt was in this up to his ears. He was tied to Carol like pansies to anisette. And maybe they were going to get married; that was the way the conversation had sounded. That tied in solidly. If Carol was the inheriting Sark wife, and if Matt had helped to fix it so Carol would inherit without waiting for Sark to have a stroke, then they married and sealed their partnership with a good, sensible marriage contract. It made sense. Because Matt was one person who had been around Sark long enough, and who was close enough to him, to persuade him he was scared to death of Albert Geysek. From then on, the whole scheme was a pipe.

I was coming along all right. I had a call in to see if Sark and Carol really had been married. When that report came in I might have some evidence. Anyway I would have something to establish motive firmly and get Framboise interested. And Framboise and his boys could go a lot faster along the road to proving who killed Sark than I could, if I got them moving in the right track.

Again, I might have to wait days or even weeks until Carol and Matt got married. That would perhaps be enough evidence of complicity to convince Framboise he was overlooking a couple of good bets, even if Carol didn't put in her claim for the Sark's estate right away. As long as Matt was left managing Sark's properties they could afford to wait to take them over formally. The management job was all Matt needed, according to him, to start getting his other angles organized.

I wanted that report from Toronto. I wanted it badly. If Tabby Gray could find the record of a marriage between Sark and Carol, I had the whole case by the short hairs. So I worked myself deeper into the bath and turned the tap with one big toe to let in more hot water and got as comfortable as a man can be. It was the best way I knew of to making the Toronto call come through.

I was right in a way and wrong in a way. I didn't get the Toronto call. But just when I was happy as if I'd never heard of John Sark, my door bell snickered at me. It snickered politely twice, then settled down to a full, steady guffaw.

I got out of the tub reluctantly. I got dressed in my best Cannon towel and trudged trailing water to my front door. I opened the door, and it was Framboise.

Instinctively, my hand went up and felt my mashed ear. I'd looked at it only a while before and it was still big and purple. Without looking at it at all I knew it was still there, because of the throb. It and my other ear made about as good a pair as an elephant and a donkey.

"You bastard," I said, and I took my hand away to let him see what he'd done to me. "Look at the goddam ear you gave me!"

Framboise blushed beet red. He didn't say anything. I looked behind him; maybe the police commissioner was with him, I hoped. But it was only MacArnold.

"Hi," MacArnold said in a voice satisfied as a bulldog full of ground top round.

"Come in," I told them. "I don't know how you can smell so good. There's beer in the frig. I managed to get it stocked up again since you two were here last." They came in and headed for the kitchen and I went to the bedroom and put on some underwear and a pair of pants and slippers. When I came back they were sitting on my good green chesterfield and Framboise had too long an ash on his cigarette. I was very short with him about it.

"Don't be mad," MacArnold said jovially. "You have been vindicated. Geysek is a free man. I made Framboise come around to tell you about it."

"To hell with it," I said. "It doesn't make me any money. All I get from it is a client who is out of jail, so he'll want me to find him a job. I knew you'd have to let him go. The only thing that will give me real personal satisfaction is to see the guy who really shot Sark in there, instead."

"W'at is it you mean, 'Guy'?" Framboise asked.

"Never mind what the hell I mean. Well, why'd you

let Geysek go? What did you find out?"

Framboise was more sheepish than any sheep you ever saw. "MacArnold came aroun' this evening. He asked me somet'ing I should 'ave thought myself. W'ose gun shot Sammy Menowitz? So, we check. You know w'at? You're right. It is the gun we foun' with Geysek. An' w'en Sammy is being shot, Geysek is wit' witnesses passing through Cornwall Ontario on 'is train."

"Sure. It was pretty plain that the first two shootings were a plant – a plant on Geysek. But Geysek outfoxed them, right from the start. He took a later train than they expected him to."

"And do you know why?" MacArnold came in. "He overslept. It was simple as that. He told his friend in Toronto he was taking the morning train to Montreal, but he missed it and had to catch the afternoon flyer. One of his Toronto 'friends' wasn't such a good pal. Because somebody tipped off the Montreal killer that Geysek was on his way."

"Yeah," I said. "Sure. Well, like I thought, you disprove one-half of the frame and the other half begins to seem a lot less logical. What other checking did you do, Raoul? Did you find Geysek's fingerprints on the gun?"

"No," Framboise admitted.

"Good. Now who are you going to arrest?"

"Inez Sark."

MacArnold carefully didn't look at me. He'd known this was coming. He sipped his beer and looked meditatively at the fringe of my rug. One string in the fringe was out of line and he reached out with the toe of his unpolished shoe and caressed it into uniformity.

Framboise didn't know he'd done anything wrong. He didn't know Inez was my client. Also, he obviously hadn't done enough thinking about the case. Or he'd done too much, and come up with the wrong answers.

"Aw, hell," I said. "I was beginning to think you were a nice guy. Now you're a bastard again. You're away off base."

"T'en you tell me. No, wait, firs' I tell you. Coincidence is strung all t'rough this case. We are hunting for the cab driver w'o carries Inez Sark 'ome from the Trafalgar on the night 'er husband is shot. Do we find 'im? Ah, no. We fin' a driver of a Diamond Cab who 'as taken a girl of Mrs. Sark's description from an 'ome on Westmount Boulevard, down toward the Trafalgar. But not direct there. On the way, she tells 'im to stop at the Castle. She gets out, she goes in for five minute' an' then comes out an' he drives her on down to the Trafalgar."

"Five minutes is a hell of a long time," MacArnold said to nobody in particular.

"Framboise, for God's sake take it slowly," I said. "Don't pull two boobs in a row on this one. Let Geysek's cell cool off for a while. Don't go crazy trying to get someone else in it."

"I don' say I arres' her tonight," he growled mournfully. I jus' ask her whether she was the one the cab-driver tol' us about. If she says no, I bring 'im to see her tomorrow, for identification. But if she says yes, in she goes."

"Why not check on her alibis for the other two killings?"

"Sure," Framboise agreed. "But I got to 'ave an arrest. I got to put somebody in a cell, an' let 'im think t'ings over, an' t'en maybe talk to me. I got no information. I get no goddamn information at all from you."

"You will," I said. "Soon. Tomorrow at the latest."

"Okay. Tomorrow. Tonight, I go see Inez."

"She won't want to see you," I said. "Her mother's giving a dinner party. She's busy."

"*Sacrement*! W'at a bad shame. Well – good bye."

"Have another beer," I said. "Hang on for a minute."

I went to the telephone and called T.A.S. Yes, there had been a call for me at my office that afternoon. A call from Toronto. Operator 18.

I got through to Toronto, Operator 18. A Mr. Gray had been calling me. But he had cancelled the call. I told her I was now calling him, so she should get him for me. She called his home. There wasn't any answer.

That was what I got for falling asleep in the afternoon instead of attending to business.

I went to the bedroom and selected a small-patterned red tie and my Harris tweed sports coat. I got dressed and came back to the living room. I told Framboise, "I thought I might have something for you. But no. Not till tomorrow."

"Hokay," he said. He got up to go. MacArnold got up too. Framboise told MacArnold, "You can stay 'ere. I didn' ask you to come."

MacArnold sat down again, agreeably. I stood up. "Sure," I told him. "You stay here. You know where the beer is. I'll go with Raoul."

Framboise sneered at me. "You! I let you come, an' w'en I go to arres' the girl you'll ask 'er to be your client. I've 'ad you pull t'at one. Once."

"I won't pull it this time," I promised. "She's my client already. Come on, let's go."

Framboise jammed his hat on his head and started for the door. His whole rear exposure had a defeated look. I followed.

He let me drive him to the Scaley summit in the Riley, and I took a childish delight in scaring the drawers off him, since I couldn't get arrested for it. A car cut in in front of me as we reeled along the Boulevard and he nearly pasted himself against the windshield when I braked. He pushed himself back into his seat and grumbled, "You shouldn' drive so fast wit'out a siren."

We got there. Framboise marched to the door. I came with him. Three boys in uniform, after they caught up to the Riley, got out of their car and lurked in the background. I waited for Martin to answer. All this in the middle of a dinner party. If his face was ever going to fall, this was the time.

His face didn't fall. He said, "Good evening, Sergeant. Good evening, Mr. Teed. Whom did you wish to see?"

"Mrs. Sark," Framboise said crisply.

"She is at dinner, Sergeant."

"T'is official business."

"Of course. I will tell her you are here," Martin said obligingly. He led us into the study. I began to wonder if I was ever going to see any of the rest of the house.

Inez, when she came, looked haggard.

I got my money's worth in first. "Inez, you fibbed to me. You did go see the Sark just before midnight the night he was shot."

She sat down woodenly, folding up like the kitchen stepladder that folds itself into a kitchen stool when you want to use it as a stepladder. "No," she said.

"Ah, what's the use? They picked up the cabby that drove you from the Archers'. He says you got out of the cab at the Castle, went in for five minutes, then came out and went on your way to the Trafalgar."

She blanched. "I went in," she whispered. "Yes, I went

up to our apartment. But there was nobody there. I rang the bell and no one came. I had a key, but I didn't use it. I went away."

"Fine," I said unhappily. "So you lied to me. You told me you didn't get out of that cab at the Castle. I can't protect you now. If you'd told me this, I might have done something. Now you've had it. Send your maid upstairs for some things. Framboise is going to arrest you."

"Oh, God!" she said through clenched teeth. I thought she was going to weep. She turned to Framboise to see if he wouldn't deny it.

"I mus' arres' you," Framboise intoned woodenly, "on suspicion of the murder of your 'usband, John Sark. You know t'at anyt'ing you now say can be taken down an' used in evidence agains' you."

"Oh, God!" she breathed again. "Russ, tell him it wasn't I. You know I didn't shoot John. I didn't know he was dead until the Sergeant told me. Don't let him take me."

I went to the bell-pull and yanked it. "I think you're innocent, and I also think you're going to spend the night in jail." Martin answered the bell. I'd have taken a large bet the dinner party wasn't getting much service just then. "Send a maid to pack some essentials for Mrs. Sark," I said. "She's going to jail. She'll need several complete changes of lingerie, nightgowns and a cosmetic and toilet kit. Don't worry about dresses. King George will provide."

His self control didn't waver, but his little pink ears turned grey and the grey shade spread slowly over his face. He loved that girl. It was s good thing he did. I'd counted on that.

He said, "Yes, Mr. Teed," in a very calm and steady voice.

We sat down and waited. Nobody said anything.

Martin came back with a small, exquisite top-grain cowhide bag. Framboise got up purposefully. Inez turned to me again.

"Russ, can't you ... "

"Nope. I can prove you're not guilty, if you're not. But I can't do it tonight. Go have a good sleep. You'll feel better about everything in the morning. Don't let Raoul keep you awake all night with his questions. If he bothers you too much, pull a faint, or call me. I'll have your mother send a lawyer around in the ..."

"Let us go," Framboise said sharply.

She got up meekly enough and went with him. He had handcuffs in his voice.

I sat there. I gave Martin time to go in and circle the dinner table once and get back out. Then I pulled the bell again.

"Through with the dinner guests?" I asked when he came.

"No, sir. I must serve the coffee in the drawing room."

"I want to talk to you as soon as you're free."

"Certainly, sir. And – Mrs. Scaley?"

"What about Mrs. Scaley?"

"I couldn't bring myself to tell her what happened."

"I'll bet you couldn't, you guilty old party. I'll tell her, but I'll talk to you first."

He started away. "And please send someone with rye and makings," I directed. "It's been a hard evening. My stummick's beginning to think my throat is cut."

He winced and nodded. I liked the wince, too. I was breaking him down, piece by piece.

A fluffy little maid brought me a decanter of rye, ice and water and a glass on a silver salver. I drank. It was good enough rye to serve in its own bottle, not anonymously.

He came back, finally. He stood stiffly in front of me.

"When you worked for Mr. Scaley, Martin, did you do any typing?"

"A little, sir, very occasionally."

"I see."

I paused and waited. Martin waited. I was trying to turn a neat phrase. I wanted something with great impact and shock value and penetrating power. Three drinks earlier, I might have done something spectacular, but now I wasn't up to it. I just said, "Martin, your son got shot this afternoon."

"I beg your pardon, sir?"

"Your son," I said crudely. "The miserable bastard you disowned years ago. You knew he was in Montreal, didn't you? You walked out on him and your wife and came here to work for old man Scaley, because things were too rotten in Toronto. You did this less than twenty years ago, not nearly as long as you told me in your first story. Old retainer, eh? Old stoolie. It's your fault Inez went to jail tonight."

He paled. "Don't say that, sir."

"I'll say that. I'll say a lot more things if you don't come clean with me. So you never heard of the Sark before Inez brought him here? You heard of him, you hoary old liar, when he married your daughter."

"No, please, sir," he said earnestly. "My daughter did not marry Sark. Or rather, John Sark would not marry my daughter. And she did not seem to care. That was one reason I left my family?"

I was tired of people talking at me earnestly. Judging by my immediate past experience, it meant they were lying. "Come on, do better than that," I said crossly. "You aren't too smart. Martin Froste? You even spelled it for me. So all I had to do was take one letter from the front and put it at the end to get Foster. The old anagram gag. Want me to tell you what else you've been doing?"

His head hung. I felt sorry enough for him that if he wanted to sit down, I'd let him. But I wasn't going to invite him to.

I said, "When you saw how Crawford and Carol were turning out, you deserted your family. I've met them and I can't say I blame you. I suppose you quarreled with your wife about the children or you wouldn't have deserted her. In any case you came here and established yourself as Martin Froste. The Scaleys took you in. They became more than your own family to you. They treated you like one of them for years. And what have you done for them? You've got Inez locked in the cooler. And here I am running around like a chopped chick trying to save her neck, and you won't help me."

"Believe me, I'd do anything in my power to help," he protested. "I know nothing that would help."

"You hoped Inez wouldn't marry Sark."

He nodded, yes, to that.

"As soon as you saw evidence it wasn't working out too well, as soon as Inez came home to mother, you thought you knew a way to break it up for good. You wrote that anonymous letter to Mrs. Scaley, telling her to look for Sark's first wife. You did that because you knew Sark had married your daughter Carol in Toronto years ago."

"No, no," he said excitedly. "I didn't write the letter. I can prove I didn't write the letter, because Sark and Carol were not married. Never, sir."

"Oh, yeah?" I said heavily. "And how do you know

about the letter at all, then? Does Mrs. Scaley show you her personal mail? I didn't realize you were that chummy."

He told me without blushing, "I regret to say temptation is too strong sometimes, sir. I caught a few words of your conversation with Mrs. Scaley on your first visit here. Then I read the letter, because of my strong personal interest in Miss Inez – and my strong, even stronger hatred for John Sark."

"Uh-huh. Well, back to your family. I've told you, your son is in town. He's selling heroin."

"God help him," Martin said piously. "I couldn't."

"Carol is also here in Montreal. She's up to her ears in these killings Inez has been arrested for."

"Then I suppose," he said slowly, "I am responsible in a way. Since she is my daughter. But, I don't see – she was his mistress in Toronto. Nearly twenty years ago. I didn't know she'd had anything to do with him since."

"She was his mistress ten years ago in Reno, too, if I'm to believe her story."

He shook his head. "I know nothing of that. I was entirely out of touch with them by then. I had done my best to forget them. I suppose Carol's path may have crossed Sark's again. But recently I supposed he was being faithful to Miss Inez. I had no reason to think ..."

"You didn't write the anonymous letter?"

"I swear I didn't. I swear the first time I saw it, Mr. Teed, was after you yourself read it. I couldn't have written the letter, because the only thing I knew of the Sark, before he met Miss Inez, was that he was a cheap swindler, who had seduced my daughter and had no intention of being honest with her. I may as well say, Sir, that I'm glad he's dead. I may also say that I had neither opportunity nor desire to kill him myself."

I reached for the rye decanter. I slumped far back in my chair. I was getting nowhere, I was tired. I was so tired, I went to sleep and then woke up again because the sleep wasn't doing anything for me, but making me dizzy. I looked for Martin and he was right there where I left him. I raised the rye decanter and drank from it like a teenager from a coke. All right, like a baby from a bottle.

"Go ahead," I told him. "Don't wait for me. Say something. Don't expect me to ask questions. I haven't any more good questions. Answer some good questions I haven't asked you."

"I don't know anything else I can tell you, Sir. I've been out of touch with my – son and daughter –" it was an effort to call them that –"for so long that I know nothing of their connections with the Sark, or with his death. I know nothing to say or do."

"And you haven't lied to me tonight?"

"I've told the truth and the whole truth tonight, Sir."

"If you have nothing further to add," I said with what dignity I had left, "send Mrs. Scaley in. But," I added, "whisper discreetly on the way that you think I'm ill."

Martha Scaley came in. She was wearing a décolleté dinner dress of some slick and shiny black material, $50,000 in tastefully assorted jewels, and an expression of annoyance at being dragged from her guests. I didn't rise, she thought. I could see her think it. She didn't know I couldn't rise.

"Good evening, Russell. I've been expecting Inez to come back to the party. Has she been here with you?"

"Has. But isn't."

"Isn't here? So I see?"

"Is in the hoosegow."

"Russell! Be sensible."

"She hash been arrested on sushpicion of murder of John Sark," I said, and my tongue was having a little trouble, and that was not good. "Anything she shays may be taken down and ushed in evidench againsht her." How did I work myself into a sentence as long as that?

"You're drunk," Martha said, uncharitably stating the obvious.

I snapped back a little. The floor stopped jumping at me.

"I'm drunk because I got Inez in jail," I said, "and it didn't do me any good."

"*You* got her in jail? Russell! Try to make sense."

"Maybe it was inevitable. Anything is inevitable, relax and profit from it. Framboise wants to put Inez in jail, I may be able to improve the occasion by getting something out of Martin. So? So Martin doesn't know anything."

I thought it was safe to try to get up again, and I tried and I could. "Besides, Inez shouldn't have lied to me," I complained. "If she'd told me the truth, maybe I could have kept her out."

I bet it was the first time Martha ever screamed at anyone. "But what are you going to do?" she shrieked.

"Get her out," I said, "tomorrow."

Scene Nineteen

SHE WAS WAITING FOR ME when I got to the door of my apartment. She was leaning against the door. She looked as if she'd been waiting a long time. There was no one I wanted less to see. There was no one at all I wanted to see just then, but her less. Less her. Lesser and lesser. You know what I mean. Or do I?

"Go the hell home," I said. "I'm asleep."

She stood aside while I scrounged for my key and stabbed it in the keyhole. When I opened the door she walked in with me.

"Please, Pamela. Go home."

"I have to talk to you," she said prettily. Maybe she looked as pretty as she sounded. I didn't know, all I could see was a blur.

I said, "Go talk to a bebop addict. You'd get more sense from him."

"Please."

I steadied her with one hand and focused one eye. The blur turned red, and then red dress, and then curve-filled red dress. On top was black hair shining, shining smooth and bright. I said, "All right, go make the strongest coffee you ever made.

I was sitting on the chesterfield when she came back. I didn't dare lie down on it. The swell was too heavy. I drank the coffee myself, without help. It may have dissolved a few amalgm fillings, but it did the trick. I could see her without closing one eye.

"Get yourself a drink," I said. "Keep it where I can't smell it.

"Thank you." She went and got a rye and ginger and came back.

"Talk now," I said. "Be engrossing. Entrancing. Or be talking to a sleeper."

"I guess I lied to you."

"That's not engrossing. It's not even news. It's commonplace."

"Eddie and I were in Toronto, not Hamilton. And Eddie was mixed up with Sark there. Sark was the one who had him jailed."

"Sure," I said. "Because of Carol. Eddie should have known better. He was too old for Carol, and not rich enough."

"I suppose so. But age doesn't make so much difference sometimes. Carol's older than she looks."

"Yeah. I gather from various sources she's been sleeping with Sark, off and on, for twenty years. And you wouldn't know she was thirty, yet. I guess she just started young."

"About fifteen, I think," Pam said. "Some do. And you'd know she was over thirty if you saw her out of her harness."

"Meow," I said. It was a nice, corny little remark and was in a nice, corny little mood. "Meow, meow, meow, meow," I said. "Out of harness she looks as young as you do. Out of harness."

She blushed. "You get around a lot."

"Sure. I'm a detective."

That finished that. We sat in silence for a while.

"Well, why'd you come, Baby?"

"I don't know, Russell," she said.

"Love," I said leering. "Undoubtedly. Too bad I'm tired."

"Don't talk about love unless you know what it is," she flared. "I've been in love. I don't expect you have."

"You don't expect I have, why?"

"Because you're a detective. Remember?"

"All my life I haven't been a detective," I maintained. "Love? Sure. I was in love. I was in love with a nice, plain little girl. Now when I think of her I have a nice plain little name for her."

"Please," she wrinkled her nose. "Step out of character. Just once. Just for a little while."

"All right. What do we talk about? Love?"

"We could."

"You can. I'll listen and try to think up some un-tough talk."

"I fell in love when I first saw him," she said.

"Sure. If it's real love, that's the only way. I guess."

"He was a lot older than I was. He was a handsome man with a fine smile and quietness about him. He walked into our store in Toronto one day ..."

"This is history. It happened years ago."

"It started years ago. It went on a long time. It went on through months of thinking of nothing else but him. Of his arms in a rough tweed jacket around me. Of the clean smell of his hair and the strength and the pressure of him against me ..."

"Hooray for sex. What was he really like?"

"Brilliant. Sometimes bitter, when he had cause. Unafraid of anyone and determined to get what he wanted."

"Egotist."

"Sure. A terrific egotist. A strong, positive guy, who

knew what he wanted and how to get it."

"So what happened?"

"In the end, I wasn't part of what he wanted."

"That can happen."

"He went on loving me. I know that. But he was too strong to stay with me when I couldn't give him anything more."

"Your fault, of course."

"I suppose so."

"Believe me, kid, it's better to be tough."

"What did it get you?"

"I wasn't so tough when I was in love. I was a lot younger."

"What was it like?"

"What is it always like? It was like being apart from the world together. Nothing was strong or real, except the bond between us. It was a short courtship, full of laughter and spring and the feeling of never having been really understood before. It was in the Laurentians. Long walks on woods trails sprinkled with sun through new leaves. Quiet nights beside lakes, long as thoughts, little rustic bars and smooth mild drinks that added nothing to the intoxication inside us. It was a few weeks out of life."

She stared at me with her eyes all dreamy.

"What was her name?"

"I've forgotten."

"Was it a lovely name?"

"It was – Nicole."

"I'm sorry about Nicole," she said, and kissed me.

The kiss became something that involved more than just our lips. It went on until it blotted out everything except body from the mind and senses – one body, two bodies; one body. We were one living, tense body.

I fought back to the surface. I held her hard by the shoulders and I held her a safe distance away. Slowly, she relaxed. That look was still in her eyes.

"You don't have to be so goddamn sorry for me," I said.

"I'm not sorry for you. I want you. I've wanted you, since I first saw you. Oh, I was angry with you for seeing me like that. But I liked everything about you. The little-boy toughness, the strength of your body that showed through your clothes ..."

"The three gold teeth in my upper denture, the Clark Gable ears."

"Do you always make women want you?"

"Only very impressionable ones."

"You're so tall and solid and smooth-muscled." She caressed the lapel of my jacket. Her hand worked around to the back of my neck and ruffled the short sharp hair there.

I could blush, or I could stay tough. "Baby, I'm not easy to make," I said. "Maybe I'm too fastidious."

"What's wrong with me?" she asked softly.

"Your filthy old uncle and his dope."

She got up and watched me with hurt eyes. I went slowly across the room loosening my tie. It landed on the rug. My shirt landed on the corridor floor halfway to the bedroom. I got into the bedroom and sat down on the bed and took off my shoes.

Pam had followed. She came up to me and stood over me. Her hand smoothed my back. "Such clear, clean skin. Golden skin." She leaned over me and her long, live black hair touched my ear. She pressed her head against mine. Her breathing was rapid. Her hand was tingling, a light touch on my bare back. She smelled bittersweet.

Scene Twenty

I WOKE UP WORRIED.

I was worried because it was still pitch dark, and I shouldn't be waking up to darkness. And I had a strong feeling someone was in the room with me. A very strong feeling; it was shaking my shoulder.

What I remembered most plainly was the last rye I shouldn't have had. It was obvious from my head. Somebody was holding me by the lower end and striking my head against some rough surface, trying to light me like a match. Somebody was also shaking my shoulder. Somebody right here beside me. Ah, yes. Of course.

"Hi," I said softly, "what's wrong, Pam?"

"Pam? Who the hell's Pam?" It was a male voice, rough as sandstone rubbing on cement.

"Oh, God," I groaned.

"It's Creep. I didn't turn the light on. I didn't want to wake you up sudden and scare you."

"You don't scare me. You gag me. What the hell time is it?"

"About four a.m."

"Well, that settles it. I'm going to sleep in a bank vault. Go turn on the light."

He stood blinking in the brightness, dressed in sharply creased slacks and a jacket that was too loud for me to stare straight at. He would have looked sharp, if he'd had a face in place of the relief map of the Rockies he carried on his shoulders.

"So, it's four a.m.," I said, "what won't wait till morning?"

"Matt."

"This is a fine time for him to turn up."

"You said you hadda see him. You wanted I should get you to him as soon as I found him. I just found him."

"Okay, okay. Go get yourself a drink in the kitchen."

I got up and had a three-minute shower. I came back to the bedroom and found my drawers under the bed, and my shoes and socks. I went through the corridor to the front room, collecting my pants first from the closet and the other things from the floor on the way. I ended up in front of the chesterfield putting on my jacket. Eddie's peashooter fell out of the pocket as I swung the jacket up to my shoulder. I picked it up off the rug, made sure the safety was on, and put it back in the pocket. Then I had a second, wiser thought. I took the gun and put the safety off, and put it back in the pocket ready for action. A .22 isn't much good, but it is sometimes better than bare hands.

I found Creep in the kitchen. "Where do I go for Matt?"

"I'll take you." He swilled the last of a drink and turned to the back door. We went through. "If I lock this up again, can you get in the front?" he asked.

"I've got my keys," I said, feeling for them.

There was his skeleton key in the outside of the lock, of course. Hanging from the safety chain was a fine, stiff wire. He closed the door holding the end of the wire outside, played with the wire for a minute, and I heard the knob on the end of the chain drop into its socket. He opened the door a crack, pulled out his wire and threaded it carefully between layers of cloth in his lapel. He closed the door, locked it with his skeleton key and pocketed the key.

"How do you do with bank vaults?" I asked him sourly.

Creep took me out the back door of the building and straight onto the mountain. Every since I grew up and got sensible I've had an aversion to Mount Royal at night. I walked behind him and kept my hand on my mechanized slingshot.

Mount Royal Park is a great wooded hummock, wild as a western story, sprung in the middle of Montreal. It's the vertical to which Central Park is horizontal, except we go Central Park one better and don't allow cars. Transportation along the winding dirt roads is by calèche, which is the word for a dilapidated old hansom-type hack pulled by a sad horse and driven by a driver who smells as if he slept with the horse. Transportation at this time of the morning was not by caleche, but by foot. We trudged.

We went along the dirt road until my ankles dragged, the black trees rising to the moon on one side and dropping to the city on the other. It was silent as a summer hotel in March. Dawn was being reluctant today, and it was blacker than the inside of a coal miner's ear.

We paused. If I still had my bearings we were directly in line with the Chalet, a large railway-terminal-like edifice perched on top of the mountain for no good reason, and we were one level below it. Several hundred wooden steps climbed from the roadside through trees to the Chalet on our left, and a steep bank dropped away on our right. Through the thin lacing of trees straight ahead came a lightening of the blue-black sky that presaged dawn.

I looked around for something solid to put my back against. There was nothing within reach, not even a tree.

Creep whistled. Then he croaked, "Okay, he's here. Alone."

A form loomed over me like a moving van over a baby Austin. The beam of a midget flashlight poked at my face and ran down my clothes.

Matt said, "Okay, Creep, blow. Teed, put your hands on your lapels. Slow, slow. Pull your coat wide open. Okay. Now lift up your coattails. Lift from the front. Yes. Turn around slowly. Okay." He gave the directions coldly, in a voice passionless as a kiss for a maiden aunt.

I did what I was told, very obligingly. Then I smoothed my jacket back in place and patted the .22 gracefully. There were a few things to be said for the little darlings. They made no more bulge than the mudguards on a new car.

"I got a gun on you," Matt said. "No offence meant. It's just that the cops are still looking for me and I don't want to see them for a while. They'll get tired of looking. I don't want to be turned in."

"I wouldn't think of turning you in."

"Okay, so long as that's understood." He turned off the flash. I moved just a foot to the west, to put off his aim if he got impatient with me.

"You wanted to see me," he said. "What for?"

"I want to find out who killed Sark. He was your boss. I suppose you'd like to see the rat get his lumps too."

"Sure," he said. "Of course I would. Don't take it wrong my not staying around to answer the cops' questions. Somebody's got to keep Sark's businesses running. If they got frisky with me and stuck me in the cooler everything would go to hell. I figure when they get the case a little better cleaned up they won't bother me too much. I'd sooner talk to them then."

"Well, I'm trying to help them get a line on a few things. Maybe I can help them clean it up. If that suits you, how about helping me? Just answer a couple of questions."

"Sure."

"When did you meet Carol?"

"Nix. Not personal questions."

"Maybe you don't know Carol used to be married to Sark."

"Maybe I don't, maybe I do. Maybe she was, maybe she wasn't. It's got nothing to do with the murders. If you want to know, I met her in the Caliban. I got an interest in that place. I developed an interest in Carol. Okay, what else?"

"When did you come to work for Sark?"

"I guess about two years ago."

"What were you hired to do?"

"Keep him safe."

"Safe from what? What was he scared of?"

"Geysek, mainly. He knew Geysek swore to get him."

"Why was Geysek so sore at Sark?"

"Sark doublecrossed him. Oh, Sark was okay to me, but he was only square if you watched. Geysek got caught by the U.S. bulls and couldn't watch anybody. So Sark didn't try to get him sprung. It meant a lot of money to Sark if he disappeared. But when it came time for him to get out, Sark was really scared."

"According to Geysek, he never made any threats to get Sark. He wasn't even mad at him. He came to Montreal to hit Sark for a job."

"Yeah. According to Geysek."

"Another funny thing, Matt. Why did Sammy get killed?"

"Oh, that was part of the same story. He was the only one besides Sark who could have helped Geysek. He held all Geysek's roll. When Geysek was pinched he wrote Sammy and told him to ship down money for his defense. Sammy showed the letter to Sark and Sark told him to forget about it. So he forgot. Who would Geysek want to shoot more?"

"Only he didn't shoot Sammy."

"Yeah? I suppose he told you that too."

"That's one thing the cops checked and got right. Geysek took the afternoon train from Toronto to Montreal. A dozen people remembered seeing him on it. The train got in at ten-thirty. And Sammy was murdered not later than nine, because that's when his body was found."

"So?" Matt sounded puzzled. "It couldn't have been Geysek who did that one, eh?"

"No. Whoever set up the frame on Geysek got a bad steer. They thought he was getting to Montreal in the afternoon, but he missed the day train. Too bad. Sammy and Butch the double, shot with the same gun, and the gun planted on Geysek. It should have been enough to hang him. But he fooled everybody. He took the Flyer."

"Your idea bein' that the same guy shot Sammy and Butch?"

"Sure. And the Sark, don't forget the Sark. He was shot with the same gun, too."

"No!" Matt said. "Honest?"

"Yep. By the same person? I wonder."

"How do you figure it?" he asked.

"I figure there was only one reason Sammy and Butch were shot. They were shot to frame Geysek. Who would want to frame Geysek? The only one I can think of is the guy who was so scared of him."

"So Sark shot them? And someone took his gun away

from him and shot him with it?"

"I don't say he shot them. I say maybe he had them shot. And then he got plugged with that gun ..."

"Could have been suicide, couldn't it? The papers said he was shot in the head."

"No gun."

"Hell, you can't tell who's going to come 'round and pick up a gun and throw it away."

"That's not all, though. Sark was shot twice – in the head, yes. But in the neck, first. That makes it hard for a man to do himself, especially when they find the shot in the neck caused death, which means it was probably done some little time before the other."

"I don't get it," Matt said flatly. "Who shot the Sark?"

"It ties in with Carol."

"Oh, you think so?" He sounded ugly. "How does it tie in?"

"Carol arranged for the Sark's hideout on the island – the place he was going to sit it out while Butch was killed and Geysek hanged for it, leaving him safe. Carol arranged that nice secluded little spot for getting rid of Sark."

"So now Carol killed him. Tell me why?"

"Because she married him a long time ago. Because he got a divorce from her that's no good in Quebec, so she gets all his property."

"So she shot him?"

"Or had him shot."

"By whom?"

"It's no secret now," I said, "she told me."

"You're a lying bastard," he said, and his gun went off in my face.

He missed me. I'd counted on that. I'd kept shifting

a bit to the right or left after each time I spoke, to make sure he couldn't pinpoint me. I crouched and got my hand on the .22 and pulled the trigger, not because I thought I could hit him, but because I wanted to show him I was heeled and make him a bit more cautious. I edged toward the steps, the steps leading up to the Chalet, the steps I knew were somewhere just to the left.

He had lost me. He didn't fire again. I couldn't hear a sound anywhere, which meant I'd lost him, too. I wished I'd put on rubber-soled shoes for this jaunt. I couldn't help scuffing the dirt a little as I edged backward. Every scuff sounded as loud to me as the tuba part in *Colonel Bogey*.

Matt might be waiting for me to make a move, or he might be stalking me. It wasn't light enough to see anything, not even a moving object. I found myself imagining the blast of his heavy gun coming again, and ducking wildly when there was actually nothing at all. My heart was banging against my ribs, trying to crack them, and my breathing was stertorous enough to waken a man sleeping two doors down the hall. I kept creeping backward easily, on the balls of my feet, hoping I was tracking down the steps.

Me and my bright ideas. So what had I got from Matt? Not a thing, unless you counted the small fact he hadn't known Sark was shot more than once. He'd been surprised to hear about the shot in Sark's neck. Which meant nothing at all.

Then my foot touched something hard and wooden. My foot groped backward and placed itself on the bottom step.

I turned and started up the stairs, still without noise. They went up for a way diagonally across the face of the cliff, then turned inward and went straight up to the level of the Chalet. I got as far as the turn in the steps when I heard him coming after me. I don't know how he got the idea I was climbing those steps; maybe I got careless as I went higher. Or perhaps it was just a lucky blind guess he made.

But he couldn't catch me now. I began to run, two stairs at a time, higher and higher up past the tops of trees, almost until I got to the Chalet.

I figured out afterward how he probably did it. He didn't see me, I'm sure of that. He could only hear me running. But, when he got to the turn of the steps, I expect he crouched and lined his gun straight up the stairway and got the right angle from feeling the slope of the rail by his hand. For a man shooting blind, he was good, or he was awfully lucky. He emptied his gun up those steps, with a roar like naval gunfire. I fell forward on my face.

The dirtiest sound in the world is the sound of a heavy-calibre bullet hitting bone, smashing and splintering and tearing it away. I lay on my face and waited for him to run up and get me. He didn't come. He knew I had a gun, and he wasn't sure he'd hit me. After a minute I heard him going away down the steps again.

I felt myself over. I began to feel a little silly. So a bullet had clipped into the rail just beside me, and I'd thought the splintering wood was my splintering skeleton.

But that wasn't right. I was light-headed if I thought I wasn't hit. Because I could still feel the force of that heavy slug striking, a force like a hard blow that spun me forward on my face. A blow on the left side. That was it; I could feel the blood. There was a lot of blood. Left arm. It didn't hurt, but it hung limp.

I felt some more. I couldn't tell how bad it was, but

somehow the arm didn't seem broken. The hole was in the upper arm, just above the elbow. I was losing blood fast, but I might be able to keep the arm. It didn't flop around and I began to hope the bullet had only grazed the bone and perhaps taken off a few splinters.

I was only a few steps from the top of the mountain. I got a rock about the size of an egg, wrapped it in my handkerchief and stuck it in my left armpit. I grabbed the arm above the wound and pulled it down hard against the rock. That slowed the bleeding to a trickle.

I had no place to go but home. Home was as close as any hospital. I started home, walking across the broad paved area in front of the Chalet.

Dawn had done it. Looking from the edge of the bluff, all Montreal was spread below, from the rich stone mansions on Redpath Crescent at the top of town, to the smooth narrow height of the Ritz-Carleton and the solid turrets of the Chateau Apartments on Sherbrooke, to the narrow busy million-signed crampedness of St. Catherine, to the railroad tracks, St. Henri's squalor, the canal, Verdun, the river. The St. Lawrence river, winding up here from the Atlantic to bring ocean ships farther inland than anywhere else in the world.

A mighty city. A mighty city for the Sark to live on like a maggot on a piece of rich fat meat. I wasn't too sorry he was dead. But the man I thought had killed him had even bigger plans.

That was Matt.

I wouldn't be sorry to see Matt dead, either.

Scene Twenty-One

IT WASN'T MUCH LIKE a bullet hole. It was more like the great gaping ragged tear a piece of shrapnel makes, like somebody had thrown a large rough rock right through my arm. I had my jacket off and my shirt off and four ounces of rye in my stomach.

It was a little after six. Doctors deserve what sleep they can get, but I needed a doctor. I called Danny Moore at his home.

I smoked three State Express and put some coffee on the stove and sucked two raw eggs to keep up my strength and he came.

He was a pink, healthy, pudgy, scrubbed young doctor, with very round eyes and a smile that never wiped off.

He said, "Cripes, what did the guy use? A shot gun loaded with rock?"

"I don't know. I'd say more likely a .45 dum-dum. Took out a hunk of flesh, didn't it?"

"And muscle. Doesn't look as though it severed anything vital, though. Come on in the bathroom and sit down."

He went to work quickly and cleanly, snipping and tidying.

"How's the bone?" I asked. "I was worried at first. Thought I heard it crack."

"Doesn't look like it, but we'll X-ray you later. Right now, all you get is a dressing and a sling. You'll live. You've had things like this before, haven't you, in the war? I mean, you'll keep quiet today and watch out for shock later on?"

"Sure, sure."

"How's your friend?"

"Have I got a friend?"

"The guy you called me to patch up yesterday. Shot in a darkroom down on St. François-Xavier. What was his name – Foster?"

God! I'd forgotten all about Crawfie. I'd found out who potted him and then never taken time to check back and see what had happened to him.

"Hell, I've been too busy since then to see him! What happened when you got there?"

"I saw your sweet little note, but I decided to fix him up before I called the cops. He was conscious by the time I got there, and a lot of people from another office were milling around. I got them out. It wasn't much of a wound. Very small hole and didn't hit anything. Then he especially asked me not to call the police, so I didn't. He said none of the others had either. He'd told them it was a very delicate personal matter and would they please omit the police. He told me it was something you were investigating, and he didn't want the cops in unless you called them yourself."

I laughed. "I can understand that," I said.

"I don't understand anything," Danny said. "For instance, who shot you?"

"It's a long story. What did you do with Crawfie?"

"I sent him home to bed. I'll look at him today."

"If you go to his place you'll have to sterilize yourself afterward."

"Okay. But the story? Give."

We went to the kitchen. We drank coffee and brewed more coffee and drank more coffee and started a third pot. All this time I was telling him. I was telling him why Sammy was killed, why the corpse in the kitchen was killed, and why his drawers and socks and shoes and shirt were stolen. Then I told him how this neat little plot by the Sark to get rid of Geysek had been turned on Sark by someone a little bit smarter, getting the Sark himself two bullets on the island. Then I took the other side of the story and traced Carol from Toronto to Reno, to Montreal, and reconstructed her meeting with Matt and how they or she or he had suddenly realized it would be wonderful if they could get rid of Sark and carry on in business themselves. I explained how Carol was doubtless the legal wife, despite the Reno divorce if there was one, and how if the Sark was bumped, she would get control of his estate. So she and Matt had worked on Sark until they got him deathly afraid of death at Geysek's hands.

Danny interrupted: "But Sark was already scared when he hired Matt. He hired him as a bodyguard."

"Whose word have I got for that? Matt's. I think Matt and Creep were hired for other duties, Creep for chauffeuring and Matt to help run the gambling clubs. He's too high-calibre a torpedo for a straight bodyguard job. I think if the Sark could tell us or if Carol will talk, we'll find out the Sark began getting scared about six months ago. About the time Matt and Carol got together, and set up their scheme, and Matt began whispering in Sark's ear that Geysek was coming to get him some dark night."

"Yes, maybe."

"Then we come to the complicated part. Sark went out somewhere and found himself a double, or had one manufactured by a plastic surgeon. That must have been just a little while ago, because it was something no one knew about and you can't keep a secret like that very long.

Sark gets this double with the idea of having him take his place, so he can go and hid out when Geysek is due in town, and wait for events to run their course. Carol and Matt have to see to it that he hides out in an appropriate place – some inconspicuous spot where he'll be easy to kill.

"Now, it so happens Carol has a brother here in Montreal. The brother – you dressed a bullet wound for him yesterday – is mixed up in a dope ring. One of the big shots in the dope ring owns an isolated island on a Laurentian lake. And Carol finds out about this island, figures it will never be traced back to her and Matt if the murder is done up there, and so – that is where Sark gets shot. It's easy to tell, but I had to go through a briny barrel of red herring to untangle it."

"So it was Matt and Carol."

"Matt's gun, and Carol's brains. Or Matt's brains, too. He had more than I thought at first."

It was eight-thirty on the nose. The phone rang.

"That will be Tabby Gray," I said. "Remember Tabby at McGill? Calling just as soon as he gets into his office in Toronto, to tell me what he's found out. To tell me he's found the record of Carol's marriage to Sark. The first link in the chain of proof."

I picked up the phone and there was the usual long-distance routine, and then the girl in Tabby's office said, "Mr. Teed? Mr. Talbot Gray calling."

"Put him on. I'm ready for him."

"Hello, Russell," Tabby said. "Beautiful morning. Two hundred dollars, please, and cheap at the price."

"One hundred dollars. This is tomorrow."

"I found it yesterday afternoon, tried your office, tried your apartment, and it wasn't my fault you weren't around."

I groaned. "No, it's my fault. I sleep too soundly. Okay. You found what?"

"It wasn't twenty years ago. It was nearer ten years ago. I wish you could be just a little bit accurate sometimes. You have no idea how much trouble you've causes me. How much useless searching through files."

"Come on, come on," I said. "You found it, didn't you?"

He told me what he'd found.

I hung up very slowly. I went back to the kitchen.

"I've pulled the biggest goddamn boob since Adam thought it would be a good idea to eat Eve's apple," I said. I told Danny.

In 1940, in Toronto, John Sark was married to Pamela Hargrove.

Scene Twenty-Two

THE RILEY WAS EQUIPPED with a gear shift on the steering column and wasn't too hard to drive with one hand. I still felt all right.

I drove right to Herbinger's drugstore. I wanted words with Eddie or Pam, I didn't care which. I wanted them soon. I got to the pharmacy about ten minutes after Tabby Gray's call, and it was open and the soda fountain was serving breakfast.

There was a different counter girl and a different soda jerk, the day shift. I went straight through the store to the dispensary. Nobody was there. I came back to the counter and collared the jerk. He was a neat boy with clear skin and thick, smoothly-brushed taffy-colored hair, a little too pretty even for the girls to go for.

"Where's Herbinger?" I demanded.

"He usually gets in before now. I don't know where he is this morning."

"How about Miss Hargrove?"

The kid smirked. "She lives with the boss. She gets away with murder – comes in when she feels like it."

"Where does Herbinger live?"

"Across the street and up around the corner on the next cross street." He gave me the number and I went back to Riley and drove there.

It was a brick veneer semi-detached duplex, very neat and new with flourishing grass in front and not a tree, one in a row of the kind you could see on any street in this neighborhood. Herbinger lived on the ground floor. I rang the bell.

Maybe he'd seen me coming. There was no answer. I tried to door, and it was unlocked.

Right then I began to get a creepy premonition. People don't leave their front doors unlocked in Montreal. Much as I hated Eddie for what he was, I began to feel sorry I'd taken his gun. I hated to think he might have been sleeping there, defenceless, when someone came in to shoot him.

The gun was still in my jacket pocket. I got it out and took the safety off. A .22 is useful when you can see to shoot. It will stop a man coming at you, if you can hit him in the face. Not in the body, but okay in the face. I held the gun very carefully and walked ahead.

The entry was fairly large and square, and leading off from it was a pretty standard living room with fireplace, chesterfield suite that I bet Eddie bought without consulting Pam, patterned broadloom and unmatched pieces of walnut furniture. Then a dining room, and a bedroom that was fixed up for Pam in rose and grey. Her bed hadn't been slept in.

The next door was closed. It was awkward to open it with the slung left arm, but I wasn't going to put the gun away. I opened the door very slowly. It was another bedroom, dark with drawn shades, and something was threshing around on the bed.

I thought at first there were two people on the bed fighting. There was enough commotion for that. Then my eyes grew more accustomed to the dim light and I saw it was one person only. It was Eddie. Eddie, almost unrecognizable, in agony. Eddie in convulsion.

I came over to his bed. I put the gun down on a table.

I wasn't going to need that gun. I turned on a light.

He was being tugged pitilessly and fiercely this way and that by horrible great contractions of unopposed muscle. His whole body was fighting itself, crumpling under the force of nerves gone wild. Great waves of tension churned across him, twisting and contorting him and tossing the bed sheets higher than Fundy waves.

Once, when I was a junior camper in a Laurentian summer camp, my best pal got polio, and we borrowed a truck from a farmer and loaded him on the back and brought him sixty miles to Montreal. I sat with him because he was my friend. He died before we got to the hospital. He died before he went through anything like this. It was bad, what happened to him, but not like this. I didn't know a human could go through something like this and stay conscious.

But Eddie was conscious. His eyes were open in his terrible twisted face. His eyes were staring at me, those softly innocent blue eyes. The eyes were not afraid. They were not agonized. They were the eyes of a fearless and proud man.

I didn't know whether he could talk. I sat down on the bed and steadied his shoulder with my good hand. It was like putting the hand on a taut, vibrating cable.

"What is it? Who did it?"

He looked at me steadily. He couldn't, or didn't speak.

"Was it Pam?"

His eyes narrowed. He tried to shake his head, and moved it a tiny distance from side to side. Then, slowly and painfully, his voice came. It was like no voice I had every heard. His throat was nearly paralyzed and the best he could manage was short, interrupted whistling gasps through his half-open mouth.

"I – have come – to the logical conclusion – of my life. I chose – my own – prescription."

"Have you left a note? Any word?"

His eyes fastened on my with an expression of ironic mirth. They said clearly, no.

"Why did you have to do it?"

"Dope. Shot – Foster. Pam –"

There wasn't much of him left. I talked rapidly. "You shot Foster to keep him from telling me about Pamela," I said. "Pam and Sark's torpedo, Matt, were hitched up in this plot to kill Sark, and you knew it. Crawfie suspected something when I told him Pam was at the island the morning Sark was killed. He suspected because he knew she never worked in the dope racket, and she wouldn't start without his knowing. He realized she couldn't have been going to the island with dope because you'd been warned away from the island that whole week by a false message through him from Mortland. She must have been going there to kill Sark. Or to help out Matt, who went there to kill him."

He was frantic in his desire to tell me something. It was almost too late. The convulsions were smoothing down and his whole body was stiffening into death. His face was inhuman now, and he could see only from one eye. But his spirit was great enough to bring his voice whistling through his stiff pipes once again.

"Pam – innocent. I – knew Sark – to go there. Checked – Foster story – with Mortland. Found – it false. Knew – Carol – Foster's sister. Found – from – her. I – killed –"

"You found nothing from Carol. You never knew her. I gave you her name, like a fool, and you gave me the story about poisoning Sark because you were in love with her. That was a lie, because really Pam married Sark and you poisoned him to set her and yourself free of him. No, you didn't know Sark was on the island. You didn't kill him. Matt and Pam knew he was going there, and Carol. Knew only because Matt was using her as a tool. And it was Pam who killed him. You know that. That's why you wanted to die."

He didn't answer that. The one open blue eye was glassy.

I pulled the sheet over his face. Herbinger was dead.

It was a hell of a way to die. If I was a druggist I'd surely know a better way. But perhaps he had turned masochist at the end, and with a guilt balance big as an ocean, decided to give himself a dose of punishment.

I wish I knew what the stuff was. I wanted to be able to run after this whenever its name was mentioned.

I wondered when he'd taken the poison, and why he'd chosen this hour to die. I wondered where Pam was, whether she'd come back to this place after leaving mine. It wasn't likely, since she had left me before five and her bed here hadn't been used. If Eddie's car was gone, that would be an indication. Of what?

At least that she was still away. Away with Matt, somewhere.

Where would I look for Matt? I'd find them both there. I'd have to find them both quickly, too, or I'd have another corpse. I expected they were getting ready to make another corpse now. A blonde corpse. The corpse of a blonde they thought had talked too much to me. The corpse of a blonde, who knew too much, who maybe thought she was due for a cut of the take.

The corpse of Carol Foster Weller.

I didn't hold much of a brief for Carol, but I didn't

want any more corpses.

I picked up my gun and got out of there as fast as a one-armed man can move.

Scene Twenty-Three

I STUCK MY HEAD into the garage on my way out of Eddie's place. His car wasn't there. I got into the Riley and broke all the traffic laws they'd thought up since Montreal was Hochelaga, getting to Carol's. I pounded up Carol's front stairs and jammed my finger on her bell. I waited plenty long enough for her to answer if she was there alive. She didn't.

I came back down to the ground floor of the building and found the service door leading into the backyard. I got out there and found my ladder. It was light enough for old one-arm to get it up against the porch roof again. I climbed. The window with the broken screen was up a few inches, as before. I ran it all the way up, took my gun in hand, and went into Carol's living room. From the living room I went through the rest of the apartment. It was empty. The bed in the one bedroom was unmade. She'd slept there, then, and got up and gone out. I wondered if she was still alive.

Then something hauled me up cold. I'd forgotten all about my shot arm, and it forced itself back on my attention by beginning to throb like Big Ben striking midnight. I had to sit down because my knees wouldn't support me. I sat down beside the telephone in the entry, and there was something I could do while I was there.

I called Framboise. I got him out of a shower. I was always getting Framboise out of showers. "I'm saving my skin," I said. "I have another corpse to report, and I'm doing it fast, while he's still warm. The name is Eddie Herbinger, druggist, address ..." I couldn't remember the house number and told him to look for it in the phone book. "The body is there in the house. It was suicide by poison. I'll make a full statement later."

"Does t'is tie in wit' the Sark case?" he wanted to know.

"Brother, it sure does. I'll unwrap the whole thing for you later today. Right now I got too many things to do. Go to bed and have a good sleep and you'll wake up with your case solved."

I hung up before he could argue with me. I sat still partly because I was pretty weak, and partly because I wasn't sure where to go next. Carol and Crawfie had both said Matt was living in a hotel suite, while he let Carol use his apartment. There were too many hotels in Montreal for that to do me any good. Besides, he was probably up and about his business by now. Maybe at the Spadina, maybe at one of the gambling clubs. There were too many for me to cruise to all of them.

Creep might know something. Anything Creep knew, he was going to tell me. He was probably at Louie Two's.

I got on my rubbery legs and made it to the Riley. Driving Riley was as easy as sitting in the chair had been, and through the arm throbbed and my sleeve began to get sticky, as though it was bleeding again, I could stand it. What I needed worst of all was a drink. That was the first thing I asked for when I got to Louie Two's, and Louie Two brought it to me himself and I stood in the barroom and tossed it down straight. His eyes wandered to my crippled arm, but he was too wise an old bird to ask questions.

Then I told him I wanted Creep.

"Sure, Russy. But Creep's tucked in for the morning. Out cold. He faded about half an hour ago and I threw him in his cot."

"I'll wake him up."

I went into the case storage room back of the bar. I found him there, asleep and snoring, on a narrow folding cot, with a torn old blanket tucked around him.

I kicked his rump, and he grunted. I kicked again, harder. It roused him. He turned his tattered face toward me with his eyes slit open and mumbled, "Wassamatter?"

"Up," I said. "Come on. Fast."

He rolled his feet onto the floor and sat rubbing his eyes. "Wheresafire?" he grumbled.

"I want Matt."

"Aw, you're off schedule. I got you Matt, already. Not four hours ago."

"I want him again. I want him now."

"Like I tole you before – I don't know where he is. I only get calls from him, here, when he wants me for something."

I showed him my gun. "Make some suggestions," I said.

"That won't get you nowhere," he growled. "I don't know."

I let the gun go off. I put a bullet in the floor right in front of his feet. "The next one goes higher," I said grimly. "Sing!"

"Honest. I don't know."

I took pretty careful aim and pulled the trigger again. I put a bullet in the fleshy part of his leg, just at the calf. It was only a .22 and maybe it didn't sting much more than a horse-fly bite, but it gave him an idea I wasn't kidding.

I'd been watching the door, but Louie Two hadn't

poked his head in. When I came in here looking for Creep I probably looked grim enough to keep him away.

I told Creep, "I'm trying to save a few worthless lives, and I need Matt awful fast. Give."

He didn't speak.

"You know Matt killed Sark, Don't you?"

"That's a lie," he said. "I don't talk for that kind of kidding."

"You'll talk for this." I got ready to pull the trigger again. I was afraid I'd have to. He had guts.

He looked me in the eyes, to see if I really would shoot again. He saw I would. "Try the Caliban," he said.

"That's better. You sure?"

"No, I ain't sure. That's where he was last night, before he went to meet you. Maybe, he's back there. If he isn't, I don't know where he is."

I went out and Louie Two was standing by the front door waiting for me. "So long, Russy," he said.

"You better go help Creepy bandage his leg," I told him. I had to get tough with him."

Louie Two looked a little sore. "I suppose you had reason, Russy. But you better tell me, good."

"You'll see it in the papers." I shoved past him and left.

There was heavy traffic all over downtown and it took me ten minutes to get from Louie Two's to the Caliban. That worried me because I was afraid my time was running out. I was getting cold chills and the throb in my arm had gone to my head and back, and the blood showed on one spot on my sleeve. And there was another thing. Creep might think to phone Matt and have him lay for me, and the longer I took, the longer Matt had to get ready for me. Or get away. On the other hand, Creep might not phone Matt, because he'd have to worry about his own life, if Matt knew who led me to him.

I drove past the Caliban and parked and walked slowly back and up its front steps. The door was locked, but it was a door with a glass panel. I waited till no one was too near me on the sidewalk, and knocked the corner out of the glass with the gun butt. It was easy to reach inside and release the lock. The breaking glass had only made a small tinkle.

The Caliban was low, but a high-class club had once occupied the building and the decor was lush. The big entry was navy blue, wall-to-wall broadloom and padded navy leather walls and navy ceiling. To the left was a door. I had to get close to it to see it was marked 'Manager.' It was a heavy, solid door covered with blue leather and studded with big silver nails. From behind it came voices.

Creep hadn't phoned. Matt and Pam were sitting ducks.

I crept close and put my ear against the door. Matt was saying, "He knows too much, Baby. He's got the whole thing figured. I don't know if he can ever prove anything on us, but I won't take any chances."

The girl said, "What are we going to do?"

"You're going to lay low until I set up a nice accidental way for him to pass out of the picture."

"God! Another one?"

"Look what we're getting, Baby. The world on a plate. It's worth it."

"What I can't figure is who told him all he knew."

"He claims you told him plenty, Baby."

"He lies, you know that. He told you that to try and make us fight. I only made one slip with him. I told him I didn't think Geysek was the type of guy who would kill

Sark. And when he started trying to figure things out, that little slip must have confused him bad."

"He knew you married the Sark. How would he find that out if you didn't tell him?"

"I don't know. I can't see it, unless he guessed. Sark and I were married in Chicago ..."

That did it. That fogged the whole picture up again. Snafu. Because it should have been Toronto. And it should have been Pam's voice.

It went on, "... married in Chicago, right after he got his Reno divorce from Pam Hargrove."

It was Carol.

I was leaning too heavily against the padded door, and it wasn't latched properly. As I fainted I fell right into the room with them.

Scene Twenty-Four

I HAD BEEN WARNED. Danny Moore had warned me. Also I knew about it myself, from experience. Surgical shock comes after a wound like mine the way a hangover comes after six zombies.

I was as big a fool as a contestant on a quiz program. All I needed to do to be safe was to bring someone with me, anyone, on this mission. But I was the big, brave lone wolf. I was Russell Teed, fearless private eye. Fearless private fathead.

When I woke up I had lots of time to think this over and grind my teeth. They were the only part of me I could move.

The office I'd fallen into was slickly luxurious. It was all navy blue, like the rest of the building, with solid mahogany furniture. There was light coming into the room from a window somewhere behind me, but I couldn't see it. I couldn't turn my head. I was bound hand and foot to solid mahogany. They had even taken my bad arm out of its sling and pulled it behind me and tied it too. The arm felt as though someone had worked it over with a meat tenderizer, but outside of that I was pretty well recovered. I should have been. There was a clock on the desk. It said seven o'clock.

Maybe there were some customers outside in the bar. If I yelled loud enough maybe one would come in and untie me. Or maybe a big fat waiter would come in and bash me on the head. My head told me not to take the chance.

After a while the door opened. I was facing directly toward it and I could see that the club was in darkness. That was funny. Carol and Matt came through the door. Carol was wearing a sleek and shiny royal blue dress not more than two sizes too tight and Matt was wearing his forehead the usual way, pulled down low over his face.

He said to Carol, "Nice of him to drop in."

"Saves us going to look for him," she replied brightly.

"Comedians, yet," I commented.

"He talks," Matt said. He came and looked me all over very carefully and then he hit me. "Shut up," he said.

He knew what to look for. He found a good place to hit. He found the ear Framboise had worked over. I shut up. I thought about the flames shooting out my ear and imagined they were hell's eternal burning brimstone and Matt was roasting in the fire. It helped, but not much.

"Who could hear a shot in here?" Matt mused.

"Nobody. Especially not if it was a shot from a .22." She opened the middle desk drawer and took out Eddie's gun. She tossed it to Matt.

He turned it over a couple of times in his hand and clicked his tongue reprovingly. "Imagine. Imagine a private peeper walking around with a little thing like this in his pocket."

"See if it works," Carol suggested.

He took the safety latch off the little gun.

"You kids have done a lot of shooting already for nothing," I told him.

He lifted the gun slowly.

"So you think Carol will get the Sark's estate? Maybe you'd be interested to know she isn't the legal wife."

"He's stalling you," Carol said sharply.

"Well, let him postpone it a little while if he wants to

suffer that much longer. Let's see if he can think up any real interesting lies." He lowered the gun.

"The Sark was sure a marryin' man," I said. "He didn't marry Carol when he lived with her in Toronto. He didn't have to. But ten years later he married Pam Hargrove there. Maybe he couldn't get what he wanted without marrying her, or maybe it was just so he could get his claws in Eddie Herbinger. But he married her. Then he went down to Reno and divorced her. In Reno he met Carol again. Maybe he got softer over the years, or maybe Carol had changed. Maybe she was smarter. So he married her in Chi, while they were coming back to Toronto together."

"You don't tell me anything I don't know," he said.

"I will, just wait. Maybe he sort of neglected to divorce Carol. Maybe she's still married to him and Inez Sark never was at all. That cuts out Inez. But in Quebec, an uncontested Nevada divorce is no divorce at all. Pam Hargrove was still Sark's legal wife when he died."

Neither of them said anything. I guess they hadn't thought of that one. They looked at each other. They wondered if I was lying.

"Makes it seem kind of silly, eh? All the big plot. All the trouble you went to, getting Sark sick-scared of Geysek so he'd go out to the island to hide when Geysek came to Montreal. All the useless shooting, shooting Sammy and Butch and Sark. For what? So Pam can take over the Sark's clubs."

"What makes you so sure the divorce is no good?" Matt growled.

"I know," I said. "But don't take my word. Ask a lawyer. Ask any lawyer."

He reached suddenly for Carol, but she twisted away

from him, her face white. "Did you know this?"

"No! don't listen to him, Matt."

"Did Pam do anything about that divorce he got in Reno? Did she contest it?"

"No. I don't know. No, or he couldn't have got it so quick."

"Jesus! I think he's right."

"Sure, I'm right."

"Look, Matt," she said wildly, "we can check it. He's likely lying. If he isn't, we can fix Pam. We can pay her or get rid of her, and ..."

"Yeah, Matt," I said. "It's a cinch. Rub out Pam. Shoot me. Bump off the lawyer I got to trace Pam's marriage, before he sees the newpapers and starts screaming. And the doctor I told the whole story to, and the reporter that was working on the case with me — take them for a ride."

"Shut up," he said. He leaned forward and hit me on my bad ear again. It felt like a grenade exploding beside my head, but it encouraged me. Better he should use his hand than the gun.

Carol was behind me. He looked past me at her. "We're through, Baby," he said softly.

"If it's true, we can get out of here. We can run for the States. They won't catch up with us."

His voice was very quiet and gentle. "They won't catch up with me," he said. The bullet sang like a snapped cable as it went by my ear. The little gun only made a pop. A man going by on the street outside would think a waiter had pulled a cork out of a bottle.

I couldn't see her. It made me very happy, not being able to see. The bullet must have gone into her head, because she didn't make a sound and she fell so fast; she hit the floor like a dropped rock.

"Four," I said. "Four this week."

"Yeah. That's the first one I ever shot with a .22. And the first time a woman. Maybe that's the way it should be."

"Why Sammy?" I asked him, "why Butch?"

"You're so goddamn smart," he smiled. "I don't have to tell you."

"And the Sark."

The smile widened to a smirk. "Yeah, Sark. The wise old Sark. You would have thought he'd be so easy? I opened the cottage door and he was sitting there with his head down. Didn't even raise his head. I put my light on him and there he was, like a blinded moose. What a pipe!"

The door was opening slowly and without noise behind him.

"It was a pleasure to shoot him," Matt said. "He thought he was so goddamn smart. You see where that puts you?"

"Sure," I admitted. "But what good does it do you?"

It was Creep in the doorway.

"It does me plenty of good. It gives me some extra hours. Hours is all I need. Why do you think I shot Carol?"

Creep had an automatic butt-forward in his hand. He was raising his hand.

"Because you're a bastard," I said, and shoved hard with my left foot so the chair crashed over on its side.

That was wise, but unnecessary like a lot of safety measures. I shouldn't have bothered shaking myself up. Creep had him before he could even pull the trigger. He brough his gun down on Matt's shoulder, putting the whole arm out of commission, and the .22 plopped out of Matt's hand onto the floor.

"I didn't hit you on the head," Creep told him. "I want you conscious."

"Let me loose," I grunted, from the floor.

"You ungrateful son of a bitch," Creep grated, eyeing Matt madly. "You shot the guy who took us out of our crummy little racket and gave us a good meal ticket. You shot him in the head when he was asleep — for his dough."

"Let me loose!" I yelled to him.

Creep untied me. He kept his gun on Matt and he kept talking to him while he worked on me. I only heard language like it once before, and that was when a Guards Sergeant-Major got his arm blown off by a mine, outside of Caen.

I got up. I couldn't move far or fast, but I could stand.

"Now, I'm gonna shoot you," Creep told him. His little squinting eyes were shot with red veins. "I'm gonna shoot you in the gut, and let you crawl around and eat carpet for a while before you die."

"Hold it," I said. "Let the law have him. You don't want to swing for a rat like this."

Creep didn't even hear me. His finger was tightening on the trigger.

There was nothing else I could do. I swung forward and kicked the gun out of his hand. It hit the ceiling before it fell.

"Thanks," Matt said. He reached into his left armpit with his left hand. It was a little awkward, but he managed. He came out with his heavy artillery. The gun Creep had knocked out of his hand was Eddie's twenty-two. Of course. In a stronger light, you could have seen my blush.

Matt looked at me. "You first."

I hit the rug behind the desk. I hit with my shot arm in front of my head, automatically, and it made me come as close to a faint as ten minutes underwater is to drowning. I could see Eddie's gun on the floor, through the kneehole of the desk. I could hear the racket as Matt's bullets came crashing through the desk like stones through streetlights.

I waited. He waited. Then I stuck my hand out through the desk and he shot at it, but he missed and I got the gun.

He shot again. I didn't hear it come anywhere near me. That probably meant he'd shot Creep. It made me mad. I stood up suddenly, and that was the last thing he expected. He was watching the lower corner of the desk, waiting for me to stick my mug around. He started, and got his gun on me, but the .22 bullet got him first. It went into him and never came out. I wasn't close enough to be sure of hitting his head, so I'd plugged his body. Maybe it hit his heart. His gun went off in his hand. That bullet broke the window behind me, shattering glass that fell tinkling to the alley below.

"Jesus!" Creep croaked.

"God! I thought I'd got you shot!" I came around the desk and saw him crouched beside a chair.

"He didn't look at me. He wanted you first."

"Good," I said. "Do something for me, will you? And then blow."

"Sure."

"Get me Carol's purse." He pointed. "It's on the floor, right beside you."

"I haven't seen her yet. I don't want to."

Creep got the purse.

I said, "There'll be people here, and cops, any minute. If anyone was near that alley, they'll think the war with Russia has started. Blow, fast. Blow town."

"I'll be seein' ya," he said. "Thanks for everything."

He left. He only stopped to get his gun. And to kick

Matt's body once.

I waited, but nobody came.

I picked up the phone and dialed the cops. I got Homicide and asked for Framboise. Framboise was out on a case. I told them who I was and they told me where he was. I wanted Framboise. I was going to deal him in on the whole hand at the finish.

I opened Carol's purse and found the paper I thought would be there.

I went for Framboise.

Scene Twenty-Five

THE ADDRESS WAS ON a side street off Ontario east. One of the thousands of side streets in the east end of Montreal with rows and rows of old stone quadruplexes, two doors at sidewalk level, outside iron stairways arching up to long balconies, two doorways on the second floor. The French architects were too economical to take up inside house space with stairways.

Framboise and his men were in the left upstairs flat. The door was open and all the lights blazed. I climbed the iron stairs and went in. There was a long, clean hallway with doors opening off it on the left. First door, living room, $119.50 burgundy plush chesterfield set, three dark varnished chairs, an imitation Axminster rug, and the *Sacre Coeur de Jesus* on the wall. Second door, walnut-stained dining room set. No rug. *St. François d'Assisi* on the wall. Third door, two Homicide men at the doorway. Mahogany-painted metal chest of drawers, ditto vanity table, ditto bed. *Notre Dame de Sacre Coeur* on the wall. Scatter rugs on the floor. Blood on a scatter rug. Framboise in the room, standing staring at a girl who sat shocked on the bed.

The girl was mute. She was yellow-white, with no blood near her skin. She had gone hungry as a child and had eaten the wrong food when she grew up, and she was thin and brittle. But she was pretty, and young. And she had killed somebody, and she was going to die. She might be dead already, except she still breathed. She had no will to hold her head erect, no power to speak or think.

Framboise saw me. "*Vous, ici?*" he asked woodenly. "*Jesu*, you are welcome to t'is one. The man was keeping her 'ere. Today maybe 'e told 'er he would stop paying 'er rent an' go back to his wife. Who knows. She shot 'im. We came 'ere an' took the gun out of 'er hand. I suppose she never hear' a gun go off before. I suppose, when she hear' it go off, she 'as not the nerve to shoot 'erself. *Jesu*."

I looked curiously at the girl.

"She don' speak English. It's all right. If I speak French, anyhow, she don' hear me."

He looked older than Moses and Aaron. He looked like a man who should have retired five years back. Maybe, he had even been crying. "An' I could 'ave been a pries'," he said bitterly.

"Through?" I asked him. "*Oui*." He said to his men, "*Gardez la fille au bureau*."

We went out together. We got into the Riley.

"Drink," I said.

"*Non*. I am on duty."

I turned the Riley and headed back west along Sherbrooke.

"I don' kid you," he said heavily. "I could 'ave been a pries'. Ma mere hope' for t'at. I was smart in school. Suppose I am a pries'. T'is little kid comes to me. She says about the man how he seduce' her, because he 'ave money to feed 'er an' buy clot'es an' get 'er a warm apartment. So 'e says 'e is leaving 'er, an' so....I have sympat'y for the kid. If I am a pries' I give 'er a stiff penitence to do, all the same, but t'at is all."

He spat over the side of the car. "But I am a cop. So w'at do I do for 'er? I'm real lucky, I don' get 'er hanged."

We drove in silence for blocks.

Finally, I said, "At least you get the pleasure of catching lugs like the one who shot Sark."

"Yeah? I catch Inez Scaley. It's fine."

"No. Not Inez. A rat."

We drew up in front of the Caliban Club. There was a big sign, 'Closed for Repairs,' over the door. That was why the place had stayed empty.

I led him inside. I found light switches. I pointed to the door of the manager's office. "In there," I said. "Dead."

He was gone a while. They hadn't emptied the stock from the Caliban bar. I located a bottle of good bonded Bourbon and splashed it in a glass. I drank it straight. I needed something raw and cutting.

Framboise came back. "*Tabernacle!*" he said, awed. "W'at a mess! You know who did it?"

"The man shot the girl. I shot the man."

"*Sacre!* I 'ope you're proud, you."

"I sure am," I said. "He killed four people I know of. This week. I hope you observed the gun in his hand. He tried to kill me, too, which makes it self-defence if you want me tried for it."

"Who is 'e?"

"His name's Matt Croll. He shot the Sark."

"Are you certain?"

"Find yourself a bottle and a glass and come sit down. It's quite a story."

I began at the beginning.

"There were two funny things about the first corpse we found, the one in Sark's apartment. I said that before, but nobody's explained them yet. First, with a dressing gown right on the hook in the closet, he grabs a sheet to come down to the kitchen. It suggests he didn't know the dressing gown was there. Second, his shirt and drawers and socks and maybe his shoes were missing. That didn't make sense. It didn't make sense until I found the second corpse, and realized Sark had a double.

"Right away you could guess the kitchen corpse was the double, because he didn't do what Sark would naturally do, even in an emergency. He didn't head for the closet and grab the dressing gown. He took a sheet. The sheet was the first clue to what happened.

"I wondered why he was shot, and why somebody tidied up after him, because he didn't take his drawers and burn them on his way to be shot. It seemed as if he was shot by someone who wanted him to be identified as the Sark. He was shot in Sark's apartment and all the clothes and belongings left there were Sark's. Now, who wanted it thought that Sark was dead?"

"Tell me."

"Sark himself. He was so scared of Geysek, he was willing to commit murder to get clear. He'd found this double, Butch, and kept the poor lug in hiding for this plan. When he believed Geysek was in Montreal, he first had Sammy shot. Maybe he had a grudge against Sammy, and in any case, it was another count against Geysek if the scheme worked. Then he got Butch and took him to the aparment. Butch and Sark stripped down to their drawers and shoes and changed clothes. That checks again, because the corpse on the island had cheap clothes except for a ritzy pair of shorts and a good pair of shoes.

"You see how good it figures for Sark. His double dead, and Geysek fingered for it. Fingered for the murder of Sark. Even if the cops don't get him, he reads in the papers that Sark is dead and so gives up and leaves town.

"So. Sark tells Butch to stay in the apartment. He leaves. Then he sneaks back in and starts raising a rumpus in the kitchen. Butch comes down, sees nobody because they're hidden, goes to the frig and — bingo."

"So it was Sark? He shot Sammy an' Bootch?"

"It could have been Sark. It wasn't. He needed an accomplice to get him out of sight and come back and plant the gun on Geysek, because they had located Geysek and the big idea was to frame him. He was to be found with the gun and hanged for the murders. So, I say, Sark needed an accomplice. And also wanted someone to do his shooting for him. He wasn't the type to do his own shooting. He'd leave it to someone he trusted."

Framboise was thinking it out. "Hokay so far. T'en it could 'ave been Inez."

"Not in character. She's straight. She might get mad and shoot somebody, but she wouldn't shoot on orders. Also, she didn't know anything about what was going on. She didn't know the Sark had a double — you saw that when she didn't know one corpse from the other. She didn't know about the double because Sark didn't trust her. Not really. He tried to seem like a clean character to her. And there's one more thing that cinches it. She has a real good alibi up to eleven-thirty — when she went to the Castle, alone, like a fool — so she couldn't have shot Sammy."

"Hokay," Framboise said. "Produce anot'er person, an' I let 'er go."

"The person Sark trusted to shoot Sammy and Butch wasn't so trustworthy after all. He followed Sark to the island and shot him, too. That came out when the tests showed all three cadavers were blown up with the same gun. It wouldn't be easy to prove, but it's logical. A lug doesn't shoot two people with a gun and then give it away for a third man to be shot with it. He doesn't even give it to an accomplice. That's a murder gun, and he wants to know exactly what happens to it."

"It is not watertight. But it is logical," Framboise admitted. "Excep' if someone hel' him up after he shot the firs' two an' took the gun from him. Or, excep' he 'ad an accomplice 'e trust very much."

"Okay, not watertight," I admitted in turn. "But it all led me to one man. It started me working on him. He's in there dead on the floor. Matt Croll. Sark trusted him and Creep Jones, his chauffeur. Either one might have done Sark's gunwork for him. But Creep was drinking in Louie Two's when Sark himself was killed."

"So? It was Matt?" Framboise was chagrined. Matt was dead. He saw the case being closed with a neat little report to the Commissioner. No arrests. No publicity. No banner headlines in the French press. He didn't want to believe me. "W'y Matt? W'at motive?"

"I couldn't figure that, either."

"T'en it's a no good case, w'at you've built up."

"I couldn't figure it at first. But what brought me into this whole mess was Inez Scaley's mother's idea that Sark had a wife before he married Inez. Somebody wrote Mrs. Scaley an anonymous letter to tell her about it. I was looking for that first wife when I stumbled over Butch's body. I found her by a roundabout route I won't take time to tell now. I found her when Geysek told me the name of an old Toronto flame of Sark's. Her name was Carol Foster."

I paused to pour more Bourbon and let Framboise get it straight. I said, "By that time I knew Carol Foster was Matt's current lay. And there it was. They'd plotted it together. As Sark's legal wife, she'd get his estate. She and Matt were going to split it."

"Where the 'ell is she?"

I stuck a thumb over my shoulder. "There on the floor."

Framboise shook his head violently. "Still no proof. No tie-in."

"I can prove by a character named Crawfie Foster, her brother, that Carol arranged the hideout where Sark was shot. I can fill in the picture by showing that Sark was scared to death of Geysek, whereas Geysek had no intention of hurting him. It's pretty easy to see they talked Sark into blowing to the island. Sark made Matt kill Sammy and Butch before he went. He got Creep to drive them to the island, so Matt couldn't kill him then. Matt had to come back to Montreal with Creep and then return to the island and shoot Sark. That's why Sark was shot four or five hours after Butch. After Matt got back to Montreal the second time, he planted the gun on Geysek."

"Guess work."

"He confessed. He told me he shot Sark. He even told me how he did it."

"He is dead."

"Check the marriage records in Chicago for 1940. You'll find Sark and Carol Foster."

He shrugged. "Anyt'ing more?"

"Every little bit helps," I said. I took out the paper I'd found in Carol's purse.

It was a marriage license made out to Carol Foster Sark and Matthew Croll.

That was the end of his back talk. I led him out the door. I put him gently in a taxi. "Police Headquarters," I said. "And don't drive too fast. He's nervous when he doesn't have a siren."

Scene Twenty-Six

I DROVE THE RILEY SLOWLY up Cote des Neiges, and the world was a better place. The warm stillness of an August night in Montreal was finer than any other time in any other place. There were trees on the mountain and stars in a cloudless black sky, and the world was going on calmly now. Everybody was dead. Matt and Carol were dead and Montreal vice could get as disorganized as it wanted to. Eddie Herbinger was dead and Crawfie Foster was scared off, and a lot of hopheads would have to take the cure and come back to life. Sark and Butch and Sammy were dead and enough rackets had died with them to make that a good thing.

Framboise had probably already let Inez out of her cell.

I came in the end to my apartment. It was cool in the corridor. I hadn't felt the heat since last Wednesday, and that meant the bad heat was over for another year. There would be good skiing between now and another heat wave.

I walked into a dark living room. My half-bought rug was thick and soft as whipped cream under my feet. When I turned on the radio some good Dixieland came from it. Bebop was dying, and Dixieland was coming back.

The world was a very good place again.

I turned on the lights. She was sitting there on the chesterfield. I don't know how she got there. Maybe she'd been there all the time. It had to come sometime. But sometime was going to be after a drink. I went and got a drink. I came back.

She hadn't said a word.

"You don't have to tell me about it," I said. "I know."

My bad arm wouldn't hold a drink. I set the glass on the bookshelf so I could get out my pack of State Express and my lighter and light up.

I said, "You were still in love with him. You were in love with him all the time, from the moment you met him, until the moment he died. That was the key to the whole thing and it took me a long time to see it. It was hard to believe. After all he did, you still loved him."

She nodded.

"Nobody had to tell you he married Carol. You knew all about that. You kept a pretty close check on him. As far as you were concerned, he wasn't really married to her at all. You wanted him still married to you."

She looked away from my eyes. It meant yes again.

"And the anonymous letter. I was pretty stupid about that. I was sure Martin had sent it. I figured Martin knew his daughter had married Sark, and because he hated his daughter and hated Sark, and because he loved the Scaleys, he was trying to help Inez out of a marriage she was sorry she made. But Martin didn't know Carol had married Sark. I wouldn't believe him when he swore they weren't married in Toronto. Funny, everybody tried to tell me that – Martin and Crawfie and Geysek – and I wouldn't believe them. It doesn't matter know. You sent the letter to Martha, didn't you?"

Her voice was harsh with a bitter emotion, the way it had been the day before in Carol and Matt's apartment when I hadn't recognized it. "It was the best way to get him away from Inez."

"How did you know about the plot to murder Sark? How did you know when to go to the island? I'll tell you what I think. You were seeing Matt. You told me a few days ago, 'I had a boyfriend; but he was stolen a few months back.' That was Matt. You were going with him because he was your approach to Sark. You even had a key to his apartment. You used it yesterday, and used it a little carelessly. You came in the apartment while Carol and Matt were sitting right there.

"When Carol took Matt away from you — mainly because she thought she had a foolproof scheme to kill Sark and get the dough — you came back to that apartment, often. You were suspicious something suspicious was afoot. You were probably the only person in Montreal, besides Carol and Matt and Sark himself, who knew Carol had been Sark's wife after you were. You hung around because your own interests were endangered. Maybe Carol was trying to get Sark back.

"But later on, you eavesdropped enough to find out she and Matt were planning to kill him, kill him as soon as Geysek came here to Montreal so they could blame it on Geysek. I'll bet you even suggested the island for the killing. It was a place you knew well and where you could control the situation. It was just too much coincidence, Carol following Crawfie and coming upon the island, ready made for her purpose, almost by chance — the way Crawfie told the story. No. You and Matt still spoke. You planted the idea in Matt's mind that the island was a nice, secluded place, the ideal place for a murder. Matt set Carol on Crawfie to secure the island for the shooting."

The bitterness was gone from her voice. Her voice admired me. "You have it so nearly right," she said. "Only I didn't eavesdrop. Matt told me about the plot. He really loved me, not Carol. He was planning to doublecross Carol after it was all over and he could do it safely and still keep control of Sark's clubs. He was going to come back to me. He told me the whole story to explain why he was living with Carol. The fool. He didn't know anything about my old marriage to Sark. He didn't know I loved the Sark, had loved him then and loved him still. He didn't understand, the way you do, Russ. He didn't realize why I had to …"

"So you watched for Geysek," I broke in. "You haunted Windsor Station waiting for him to arrive in town. When he came you knew Sark would be going to the island. But you knew there were things to do first, like killing Sammy and Butch, and so you started for the island to get there before he did.

"You had it all figured out. You'd sent the anonymous letter to Martha. You were going to get the Sark away from Inez easily enough. When you went to the island you were waiting for him to come, so you could talk to him. You would tell him Carol and Matt were planning to kill him. You wanted to convince him of that. Because if he believed you, he'd take you and run away from all of them."

"That was what I hoped." Her voice was dull and dead.

"So you got out to the island about midnight. You hid the car in the brush. When you got into the car in the morning it was very hard to start. And it looked as if it had been there for a long time, not just for an hour."

She nodded.

"You didn't want to arouse anyone's suspicions, so you left the boat there on the shore and swam over to the island. I always thought you were going to meet someone you loved on that island. It was fairly obvious. But you took along a gun. You're a strong girl. You could swim with one arm, holding a gun up out of the water to keep it dry. Maybe you had the gun to give to Sark. Maybe you were afraid you'd have to use it on Matt. But you had it.

"When you got to the cottage you lay down in the back bedroom to wait. You pulled a blanket over you and forgot to fold it up again."

The drink was gone. My throat was dry and painful. I had to keep on. "Sark came, and since Creep rowed him to the island, Matt had to go back to Montreal and return before he could kill him. So you had hours to argue with Sark. It was only two when he got to the island.

"You made love to him. You told him how everyone was faithless, except you. You told him Inez was through with him now. Maybe you convinced him he was in danger, but you couldn't make him want you back. Too bad, for him. You got him out of the cottage, somehow, before you shot him. There was no blood in the cottage, and no bullet, but Matt's. You shot Sark through the neck and dragged him back inside and put him in the chair."

I found an ashtray and butted my cigarette.

Her voice sank to a whisper. "The love all turned to hate," she said. "He'd never loved me. He'd only used me to get Eddie to work for him. I thought he really loved me always, and only left me because Eddie tried to poison him. I wanted to make up to him for that. That was why I tried to save him from Matt. When I saw what he really was, I couldn't even leave him for Matt to shoot."

"But Matt did shoot him. Matt came to the island before you could get away. He came to the cottage and flashed a light on Sark and shot. Not knowing Sark was already dead. That was your big piece of luck. Matt's was the only bullet they found. It explained so much nobody looked further.

"You hid until Matt went away. Then you threw your gun in the water and swam to shore. Too bad I was there. Too bad, I could tell your car had been there most of the night. That didn't tally with any of the stories you told. Neither did the way you were dressed. Yeah, too bad. I'm the only one who could ever connect you with it."

She stood up. There were tears in her lovely eyes. She held out her arms to me. They were wonderful, strong, supple arms. The glistening eyes were full of the only love she had left. Me. Her body was hot and young and eager, and she wanted only me. She didn't have to say that. Her whole being said it as she came slowly toward me.

I backed away from her. The look on my face told her what I thought of her.

"Get out," I said. "I didn't turn you in, but I don't want you. I don't care where the hell you go, but go."

Very slowly, her arms dropped to her sides. Her head sank. She turned and went.

For two days I didn't know where she'd gone. I didn't know whether to tell anyone about her. Framboise was satisfied with the solution he already had. It would be hard as hell to persuade him another one was true. Anyway, who would convict her?

I wasn't mad at her. I don't know that I even blamed her, really. I just didn't ever want to see her again.

Murder is murder.

It turned out she took the same way as Eddie. At the end of the two days, I found out what she'd done. They fished the most beautiful lower lip in the world, along with the rest of the almost unbelievable body, out of the St. Lawrence River. She'd only been in the river twelve hours, so I like to think it was her own thoughts and not what I'd said that drove her to it.

That was the end of Pamela Hargrove.

Sometimes I still wish I had her back in my bed. But I'm glad she and all the other dead ones are out of my life. And I was glad when the Mounties got the goods on Mortland and Crawfie and put them away.

All I got out of it was my thousand dollars and a dinner with Martha Scaley.

THE END

Véhicule Press
www.vehiculepress.com